# Austenistan

# Austenistan

Laaleen Sukhera

BLOOMSBURY
NEW DELHI • LONDON • OXFORD • NEW YORK • SYDNEY

First published in India 2018



ISBN 978 93 86950 26 0
4 6 8 10 9 7 5 3

Bloomsbury Publishing India Pvt. Ltd
Second Floor, LSC Building No.4
DDA Complex, Pocket C – 6 & 7, Vasant Kunj
New Delhi 110070
www.bloomsbury.com

Typeset by Manipal Digital Systems
Printed and bound in India by Thomson Press India Ltd.

*"There is no charm equal to tenderness of heart"*
—Emma, 1815

For my daughters Misha, Eisha, Amal

# Contents

# Foreword

200 years after Jane Austen published her most famous works from her cottage in Chawton, in the South of England, her novels are enjoyed by a global audience from many different cultures and walks of life, each able to connect to her stories in their own way. Having grown up in Chawton House, the grand country home of Jane's brother Edward Austen Knight (my fourth great-grandfather), where my family had lived for generations, I am familiar with the surroundings, family structures and traditions of the landed gentry. Almost every Austen reader I speak to can clearly relate to the essence of her characters, skilfully painted in often just a few carefully chosen words of dialogue. In some countries readers experience similar predicaments to the women in Jane's novels, with limited rights, independence and earning opportunities. Others can relate to the social norms and family expectations around the finding of a suitable husband!

Whatever the personal connection, Jane's work brings people together in a mutual admiration and enjoyment of her work. Academics, appreciators and fans regularly gather at one of the many Jane

Austen societies, events and meetings around the world, or belong to one of hundreds of online communities dedicated to Jane. The Jane Austen Society of Pakistan is one of the newest societies and I am excited to see Jane's work celebrated in new territories. Thanks to the power of Skype, I have had the pleasure of getting to know Laaleen Sukhera, the Founder of JASP, and gained a greater insight into Jane's relevance to the Pakistani culture.

*Austenistan* is an anthology inspired by Austen's writings, characterisations, and settings, written by women who, in many ways, have far more in common with Jane's world than modern western readers. It provides fictionalised snapshots of Pakistani society amid humour, drama, and romance, all written by women who have ethnic, cultural, or geographical ties to Pakistan. Edited by Laaleen, *Austenistan* celebrates the legacy of Jane Austen, who, despite the cultural expectations of her time, completed six novels that still touch the lives of millions today.

Jane Austen is an inspiration to us all and I was inspired by her phenomenal legacy to start the Jane Austen Literacy Foundation to raise money to buy literacy resources for communities in need. Literacy is fundamental for learning and I am delighted to be working with Laaleen to establish the Pakistan Chapter of the Foundation to fund literacy resources for Pakistan, where an estimated 45% of the population is illiterate. Reading and writing empowers individuals to participate in society and achieve their dreams.

Caroline Jane Knight
Founder and Chair
Jane Austen Literacy Foundation
*Raising funds to buy literacy resources, in honour of Jane*

# The Fabulous Banker Boys

**Mahlia S Lone**

*"The business of her life was to get her daughters married"*

—Pride and Prejudice

Jameela Baig looked at her reflection in the mirror of her armoire and wondered at the woman staring back at her. Pulling her skin taut, she could still recognise her youthful self, but once she let go, her resting bitch face was that of a stranger. She couldn't remember when she'd developed this peevish expression with a downturned mouth. Her eyes were droopy, which was unavoidable—she couldn't afford the anti-ageing treatments her friends indulged in. Even if she could, no doctor could give her back the naughty sparkle she'd been known for. She sighed deeply. *When did I become this woman? How?* She remembered being an excited young girl full of hope, but it had been so long ago that she wondered if anyone else remembered, or if they only thought of her as a tired, middle-aged woman ground down by worrying about money and the fate of her children. She had four daughters, and not a single son despite all the prayers she'd offered and all the shrines she'd visited. She loved them dearly, and knew she shouldn't complain because for the first ten years of her marriage, there had been no children at all. Still, she couldn't help but feel that fate had been a little cruel. And then, there was the matter of her husband.

Javed Baig had been full of promise when they married. Born to a comfortable landowning family from a dusty town in rural Punjab that had remained unchanged for centuries, Javed had passed his Civil Service exam just before she met him. Jameela had been enrolled at Kinnaird College, which was, then, the only suitable place for a young lady to seek an education. She had been thrilled when her parents received the marriage proposal from the well-respected Baigs – a piece of luck she owed to her fair face and the machinations of the matchmaking busybody known as *rishtay waali amma*, who Jameela's mother had enticed with her own 24-carat gold bangle.

The Baigs were well-connected so Javed got a plum posting in Lahore with a government bungalow, which she smartened up with the furniture she had brought in her dowry. The young couple's future looked bright and rosy. Both families waited with bated breath for news of a son and heir. They waited and waited. Jameela found herself pregnant a few times but couldn't, it seemed, carry a baby to full term. Desperate, the couple consulted fertility specialists all over the country and Javed started selling off land in his backwater hometown on the cheap to fund treatments for his wife. Javed and Jameela became consumed with only one thought: a son.

At work, his wily peon would bring him business cards of wealthy men who required him to turn a blind eye to whichever law they were breaking in exchange for a generous bribe, but Javed would irritably wave him away, fearing that Allah may not listen to his prayers for children if he transgressed in any way. Uncooperative in the ways of the world, eventually he was relegated by higher-ups to working as a paper pusher in a dead-end bureaucratic position.

Every time Jameela miscarried and cried hysterically, Javed disconnected from reality a little more and distanced his wife by shutting himself off in his study. He didn't know how to comfort her. He was eaten up with guilt to begin with but as time went by, it became easier for him to isolate himself from her. It almost became habit. Then, miraculously, after they had nearly given up all hope, Jahan arrived, followed in quick succession by the next three, all girls. By this time, they were too grateful and too busy taking care of their young brood to care that the requisite son still eluded them.

On Javed's retirement, the Baigs moved to a rented house in Garden Town, a once-up-and-coming Lahore neighbourhood which the property boom had passed by. Once well-maintained, and as green as its name suggested, Garden Town had since grown decrepit with cobwebs of electric wires hanging from poles and old houses with peeling paint lining the potholed streets. Inside, the drawing room was still decorated with the good furniture she'd brought in her dowry—heavy, carved woods that lasted, along with some crystal objets she'd bought over the years. The part of the house reserved for the family's own use had cheaper furniture they'd bought more recently, ranging from modest pieces in less expensive wood to imitation wood. Javed's salary, and now his pension from the civil service, was a joke, so piece by piece, over the years, they'd sold off all his family land. With all the bills, tuitions and expenses of a family of six depending on a single income, their household budget was too tight to spend on interior decor, let alone buying somewhere new to live. They'd have had their own property if they'd thought to buy one while Javed was still living in government housing. But property prices in the city were too high now, especially in the affluent new neighbourhood of Defence where their friends lived, with all the modern luxuries of underground wiring, regular garbage pickup, well-designed bungalows, and perfectly paved roads.

The girls' weddings still had to be paid for and their trousseaus purchased. Times had drastically changed since their own wedding when one could get away with dinner for a couple of hundred people and dressing the bride in a gold-thread-embroidered bridal outfit and gold jewellery. Nowadays, every component of a wedding was a Bollywood production. They could barely afford their daughters' school and college tuition.

The girls' private schooling was the one luxury that Jameela and Javed both insisted on for their daughters – Javed because the idea of stupid children filled him with horror, and Jameela because she knew that if they were to make good matches, they must rub shoulders with the daughters of affluent families like the ones that went to the all girls' Grammar School. It was a necessary expense and one which their birth entitled them to.

*No matter, they are pretty girls, like I was, and vivacious,* she sighed. *We will manage something, Inshallah.*

She gazed at the four bent heads poring over their smartphones. Twenty-year-old Jahan was angelic in looks and temperament, docile and good-natured, full of the sort of sweetness that men found appealing. Then came Elisha, her father's pet, with bucket-loads of independence, spirit, and strong personality. *No man likes a headstrong and blunt wife,* she thought. However, she had to admit that the girl knew her own mind and wasn't needy. *I must teach her to at least appear more subservient and pliant.*

Her youngest two – Khadija and the sixteen-year-old baby of the family, Leena – were shrieking.

'Give me back my phone,' screamed Leena, clawing the air as Khadija held the phone high over her head. 'Mama! Tell her to give me back my phone!'

Spoilt by her parents and looked after by her older sisters, Leena wasn't the most mature 16-year-old.

Curvy, fashion-conscious, and skilled with makeup, even on her limited budget, she looked older when she dressed up. It was proving to be a dangerous combination.

'She's texting a boy again, Mama. That Dilawar.' Khadija said, referring to a good-looking and thoroughly spoilt young man who had been making his interest in her known recently. A few years older than Leena and the scion of a rich political family, Dilawar drove around town in a brand new Porsche Panamera and had just been expelled from an American college for cocaine possession. His parents, insisting the university had cooked up the charges, felt that it was just as well that he was back since he had to learn the ropes of the family business anyway. In reality, learning the family business meant he had nothing to do and money to burn, so, he spent his time throwing parties and chatting up whichever pretty girl caught his eye. There were lots of takers.

The glowing message read: 'What's the plan? Want to do lunch at Cosa Nostra?'

*Hmmm, the catty aunties will see her, assume the worst and she will get a 'fast' reputation,* thought Jameela. Not one for letting an opportunity slip though, she hit on a compromise.

'Take your sisters with you and you can go.'

Elisha looked coolly at her mother. 'You know we can't control Leena, Mama. She'll want to take off with Dilawar for a spin after lunch. You know how persuasive he can be and she doesn't listen to us when she's all goo-goo-eyed. You need to be stricter with her.'

'Oh, hush,' said Jahan, the family peacekeeper. 'We'll take care of her, Mama.'

'Thank you, Mama, you are the best and the coolest!' Leena purred, throwing her arms around her mother and giving her a resounding kiss on the cheek.

*I am cool*, Jameela thought, heading towards the kitchen to order tea, when her own phone started ringing. It was nowhere near as sleek as her friends' latest smartphones but it had been bedazzled by her younger daughters. She heard her sister Aneela's high-pitched voice at the other end.

'Jameela? Did you get your cards for Momo Mirza's daughter's wedding?' Aneela said, not bothering with a preamble. 'You must go. There are going to be so many boys there for your girls, those Mirzas know everyone! I've already heard about two eligible men who are coming from Dubai. One is the son of the Dars who live in that big 12 kanal house in GOR and is visiting from Dubai. The other is related to the Corps Commander of Lahore, General Humbhi, and they're both bankers. Have you heard?'

'*Apa*, that's very exciting, you know I don't sleep at night, worrying about what will happen to my girls. I had to take an Ativan every night this week. We haven't had any invitations yet because you know what Javed is like. Day and night, I tell him to be more sociable, to make friends who might be useful to the rest of us, but does he listen? No! You know how stubborn he is.'

'Well, my nieces are such pretty girls that they will easily get good marriage proposals, but do try and get invited to the Mirza wedding. I have to go now. Anwar is calling me,' and she hung up abruptly. Anwar, Aneela's lord and master, owned a supermarket known for its array of imported, or smuggled (depending on who you asked), goods. The whole fashionable world bought its supply of smoked salmon, Brie and Dove soap there, but the society set still turned up their nose at him for being a glorified shopkeeper. He was doing very well off their money though, and Aneela was more than satisfied.

'Javed, sweetie,' Jameela cooed, sounding quite like Leena, 'such eligible boys have arrived from Dubai for the Mirza wedding! You must make sure we are invited so they have a chance to meet our girls.'

Javed was sitting in his study clicking on his massive, outdated desktop computer. He hastily minimised his browser window to conceal the pornographic site he had been on. Jameela knew about his pastime, but shrugged it off. She had far too many things to worry about.

'Why must I get us invited?' he asked wearily. 'These boys are here to attend a wedding, not to meet our daughters.'

'Jaadu, how can they like our daughters if they don't get to see them? I'll bet all the other women have had designer ensembles made for their girls for this wedding. It's so competitive nowadays. Never mind, I know we can't afford that, I'll take something old from my trousseau and reapply the embroidery on new fabric.'

Javed winced at being reminded of their straitened circumstances, but Jameela rattled on.

'They are such lovely girls,' she continued, 'that they will stand out from the others. You must go and meet Mirza and congratulate him. He will definitely invite us then.'

Javed held his ground, 'I don't want to cosy up to him just for an invitation. If only you were as interested in the girls doing well in their studies as you are in them getting married, they would not need to depend on finding husbands to provide for them....' His voice trailed off as his irritated wife slammed the door shut in exasperation.

The next day, Javed returned from his Friday prayers as chicken *qorma* and *chappatis* were being brought to the table for lunch.

'Guess who I just met?' Javed said, coming into the room with a spring in his step, clearly feeling quite pleased with himself.

'How do I know?' muttered Jameela, still sulking from the night before.

'Jehangir Mirza with the two boys from Dubai, they were at the mosque for *Juma* prayers. I went to the mosque in his neighbourhood, hoping to run into him. Aren't you pleased?'

'Hmmm, did you congratulate him?' Jameela said, not daring to hope.

'Not only did I congratulate him, but he also asked me if we received our wedding invitation. He gave it to our neighbours, the Laeeqs, to pass on to us.'

'Those Laeeqs! Always so sneaky, I'm sure they kept it on purpose. Their daughter Shazia, *bechari*, is so plain compared to our girls.' Jameela said. 'Even though she's the only daughter and will inherit property,' she added with a tinge of resentment.

He produced a thick cream envelope containing a stack of gilt-edged invitation cards from behind his back with a flourish.

'Oh, Jaadu, you're the best,' squealed Jameela. 'Girls, girls, look what your father has brought!'

The girls trailed into the room. The youngest two were giddy with excitement, and immediately started discussing potential outfits. Their *mehndi* outfits must be particularly eye-catching. It would be so much fun. They would dance the night away and take a million selfies! Jahan also looked pleased, but Elisha acted cool though she was also excited to be going to one of the year's biggest society weddings. While they would always have some cachet as a former landowning family, they couldn't afford to repay anyone's lavish hospitality, and invitations had dwindled. Jameela was going to make sure this wedding wasn't a wasted opportunity.

That weekend when the Baig family piled into their trusty white 1999 model Toyota Corolla, the girls were dressed to the nines. Care had taken the place of expense, and their clothes, made by a local tailor, looked as good as anything seen in shop windows. More than their ensembles, it was their youth and their barely suppressed excitement that made them radiant. Jahan was wearing a white *gharara* spangled with silver-gold *ganga-jamni* embroidery from her mother's trousseau, channelling a Mughal princess from a period drama. Elisha was pretty in a pale pink *kurta pajama* with a delicate ruby jewellery set in yellow gold, her dark, lustrous hair swishing at her waist. Khadija and Leena were vibrant in lemon and lime, traditional *mehndi* colours, with matching glass bangles tinkling on their slim wrists.

Jameela had chosen a gold organza outfit for herself, a trifle garish at her age, but she had never been one for subtlety. She had applied bright red lipstick and her heavily highlighted blonde hair had been backcombed into a mini-bouffant. One could tell that she'd been pretty in her youth, but she couldn't afford a dermatologist's fees for regular fillers and Botox like her friends. She covered up her skin, a little saggy and sallow from menopause, with a thick layer of foundation, powder, and rouge, that only seemed to enhance her wrinkles, and age her beyond her years.

The Corolla drove up the congested street of the bride's family home with bright, white spotlights illuminating the way, as few of the public streetlights were functional. A huge yellow generator, parked in front of the house, roared and groaned in turn. Cars snaked around the house, with wedding guests being dropped off by chauffeurs at the entrance. The pulsating beat of the *dhol* could be heard even at a distance. Javed dropped his family at the gate, thronged by guards, and drove off to park his car in a vacant plot of land near the house. Once inside, he spent his evening with old family friends and didn't see the ladies again until it was time to leave.

A lush canopy of red roses interwoven with twinkling fairy lights decorated the entrance, flanked by massive wrought iron candelabras. The entire house was covered with white fairy lights. Guests could tell that the Mirzas had spared no expense in hiring a fashionable event planner to handle the décor. An all-encompassing velvet marquee covered the sculpted garden, converting it into a makeshift ballroom. An illuminated dance floor blinked with coloured disco lights in the centre, below a contrived floral ceiling lit by myriad LEDs. A flower-bedecked platform bearing a traditional carved wooden swing for the bridal couple had been placed next to one side of the dance floor, so that the two could watch the action. The younger lot had been practicing choreographed Bollywood dance routines for a month.

Round dining tables shrouded in white table cloths and accompanied by acrylic chairs dotted the back of the lawn that was edged by buffet tables. These would later be groaning under the weight of a vast array of elaborate entrées and sides. Golden satin sofas were lined up for the expectant guests, the front ones reserved for the all-important bridegroom's family. Massive flower arrangements were perched on tall cocktail tables and added height in the mingling area. A tall mirrored bar, upon which bottles of Black Label, Grey Goose, and French table wine were proudly displayed, had a throng of early-bird drinkers in front of it, loath to end their happy hour anytime soon. The bartenders in their starched white uniforms already appeared a little sozzled as well, mixing drinks for the guests while sneaking shots for themselves behind the bar.

The giggling girls sauntered off to join their friends, where they stood possessively by the colourfully decorated henna platters dotted with tiny birthday candles. The girls chosen for the all-important role of carrying the henna platters and walking alongside the bride as part of her entourage were considered the bridesmaids and had all eyes on them as they carried out their special tasks. Enjoying their time in the limelight, they pouted and posed for selfies for their Instagram and SnapChat accounts, some being picked up by glossies always on the lookout for pretty faces at society weddings.

'Look, look,' Aneela said to Jameela, who was blowing air kisses to her acquaintances. 'Those are the boys from Dubai I was telling you about.'

Tall and handsome, though with the hint of a frown, Faiz Dar was dressed in a black *kurta shalwar*, and had a physique that suggested regular visits to the gym. Saif Bhatti was leaner, of moderate height, and had an open smile. He was dressed in a snowy-white *kurta shalwar*. The two young men, who had unwittingly become the talk of the town just by showing up, were chatting while watching the groups of chattering girls parading for their benefit, Dar with slight disdain and Bhatti with some interest.

The bride's brother, their friend, Kemal Mirza, pointed out various personages to them, particularly, the more attractive girls. He wanted to show all his out-of-town friends, some coming from as far as London and NYC, that his city was also sophisticated, enjoyable, and boasted of some of the finest looking young women in the world. Faiz, who had grown up in Lahore, didn't look very impressed.

'Look, the Baig girls have arrived. Jahan and Elisha are pretty hot! That one with the really killer figure is Leena, she's still way too young. But you should dance with the older two, they're attractive,' Kemal said to his friends, sotto voce, as the sisters stopped near them to kiss some of their friends hello.

'I don't do *bhangra*, sorry,' said Dar, even though he enjoyed dancing, he was just so sick of incessantly being set up. 'Yeah, Jahan's quite pretty, but Elisha is just OK. She isn't hot enough to tempt me.'

Elisha was standing near enough to hear Dar voice his opinion, but acted as though she hadn't, and laughed with much fake mirth at her friend

Shazia's joke. *What an arrogant prick*, she thought furiously, nostrils flaring. *What's his problem?*

She shot him a look of utter disdain just as he looked up and caught her eye. Realising she'd overheard his offhand remark, he felt his face heating up. She looked away and laughed at what her friend was saying. *A look of disdain from a single woman? Could it be that she wasn't interested in him? The situation was unheard of.* He smiled, in spite of himself. When he looked up again, she was gone. He found himself looking for her through the crowd.

Kemal beckoned a chubby guy dithering at the edge of their group hoping to join them. Chughtai was a balding bachelor in his late 30s with a distinctly seedy look to him and an over-friendly manner.

'Kemal! How are you, *yaar*? Have you seen Elisha anywhere? My cousin always runs off when she sees me, she's such a shy girl. If I didn't know any better, I would think she didn't like me.' He laughed raucously. 'She's pretty hot now that she's all grown up! *Yaar*, are you from out of town?' he said to Faiz. 'I haven't run into you anywhere before, I am sure, and I go everywhere!' Chughtai said, putting an arm chummily around Faiz's shoulder. Seeing the latter frowning, he thought it best to remove it. Faiz walked off without answering.

Walking through the party, Faiz was mystified to find himself still looking for the girl who'd shot him that look. He found her standing near the dance floor with a gaggle of young women, all of whom smiled as he approached.

'Faiz, *beta*,' bellowed a matronly woman dressed to the hilt in all her finery. 'There you are! I've been looking all over for you. Why aren't you dancing and enjoying yourself like all the other young people?'

Not waiting for him to answer, Polly, as she was known to young and old alike, pulled her oldest friend's son roughly by the hand and shoved him towards Elisha. 'She isn't dancing either, I don't know why. Go on, you two!' she said, high-handedly. They gently collided.

'Er hi…I'm Faiz Dar. Sorry, but it looks like we're dancing together. Polly doesn't take no for an answer and will just harass me till I do what she wants.'

'She just wants you to dance, she doesn't care who you dance with,' Elisha said.

'She literally pushed me at you,' Faiz said, raising an eyebrow and risking a smile.

'I'm sure there are plenty of girls who would dance with you, but I'm not one of them.'

Faiz looked at her, unsure as to whether she was being serious or mocking him.

'I really don't dance with people I don't know or haven't been properly introduced to,' she elaborated. 'Especially if they think I'm just OK. I have some standards!'

'I suppose I deserved that,' Faiz said, looking so sheepish that Elisha laughed in spite of herself. She looked at his outstretched hand and slowly placed her slender palm in it.

To the envy of the girls around them, they began dancing to the remix of a soulful Rahat Fateh Ali Khan ballad. Faiz was rhythmic but restrained compared to the brisk young men that dominated the dance floor. Fuelled by their heavy drinks, they were leaping with such exuberance that the dance floor trembled.

The worst offender was a happily high Chughtai who could be seen bopping up and down vigorously on the floor, his arms and legs flailing in multiple directions. He interspersed this with loud whooping. His *kurta* was unbuttoned to reveal twin mounds of hairy flesh—B-cup moobs, and a gold chain that lay nestled in the valley between. Tiny beads of perspiration created a misty halo around him as his cloying cologne mingled with his wafting body odour. Shazia Laeeq, his dance partner, looked relieved that she wasn't dancing alone at the periphery for once.

'So, you're from out of town, aren't you? How do you find Lahore?' Elisha sought safety in asking the generic question that every visitor is asked, as she swayed sensuously to the music.

'Well, I grew up here, but I haven't lived here since I was eighteen. It's been a decade already.'

'It's probably still the same in most ways, isn't it…where'd you go to university?'

'Exeter in England. Then I started working in Dubai to be near enough my parents without giving up my independence.'

'Didn't they want you back home, though?' asked Elisha with surprise. Most people who inherited sizeable incomes returned to their parents' homes after acquiring polish overseas.

'See, that's where I draw the line. I wanted to make it on my own, not take the easy way by joining the family business.' Faiz was unused to speaking so easily, especially to a girl he'd just met.

'Yes, I understand,' she said. *He's not such a dick after all.* 'I want to make my own way too.'

They were oddly comfortable speaking to each other, yet not relaxed for being hyper-aware of the other's presence. A little quickening of the heartbeat could be due to the physical exertion of the dance, their proximity magnetically pulling the two in a seemingly synchronised movement. The rest of the world dimmed and they felt a golden otherworldly glow around themselves, perhaps due to the ambient lighting.

'You mean you want to find your own husband and not have an arranged marriage?' he said with a smug, tight smile as if he'd figured her all out.

'No,' Elisha said sharply. 'I want to have a career, a proper career. I've always enjoyed reading and writing—I grew up surrounded by my father's books, which I read cover to cover several times,' she explained passionately. 'I love stories, writing, and want to become a journalist. I know it doesn't pay very well, but that's what I'd love to do: become a professional writer. I'd go crazy trying to run a house!' She smiled. 'My mother hates that I don't want to be a housewife, but I keep telling her the world doesn't revolve around men any longer.'

'Oh, I don't know about that. Trust me, I'm not exaggerating when I say I've been pursued by many matchmaking Aunties, and got hit on by plenty of single girls on this trip.'

Elisha raised her eyebrows at his arrogance.

'I could be the serial killer from *American Psycho* for all they know,' he continued, 'just as long as I'm single, it seems to be enough for them. Most don't even try to be subtle. I wish I could swipe people away in real life as easily as on Tinder. Takes all the fun out of the chase.'

'Oh, really? Maybe you should take it as a compliment that they find you so irresistible and think you are the most eligible man on Earth,' she replied, with an edge in her voice.

'I *am* the most eligible man on Earth,' Faiz said, drily. They both laughed.

'Saif and I are here for a week. Are you going to attend the other functions?' Faiz found himself asking to his own astonishment.

She sighed. 'Well, I'm expected. I'm not sure why weddings are so never-ending that the bride and groom are left drained and exhausted at the start of their new life!' she stopped and flushed, remembering how close Faiz and Kemal were. 'I shouldn't complain, of course.

It's a beautiful wedding, and it was very kind of Uncle Jehangir and Aunty Momo to invite us.'

Faiz laughed at her refreshing artlessness.

'It's OK, I totally understand. It can be a bit much. I'm only here because I've known Kemal since our Aitchison days. We always got called in to the headmaster's together. He'd kill me if I missed any of his sister's wedding. Well, I'm glad you're going to be here.'

'Let's see,' she said, fully intending to be at every event but not wanting to give him that reassurance.

He smiled. Finally, a girl not bending over backwards to see him again.

The song came to an end and Dar put his hand on the small of Elisha's back to guide her through the crowd. Nearby, Chughtai was still prancing up and down. Just then, he stomped on Shazia's toes. The poor girl let loose a cry of pain that was mercifully drowned by the music, and skipped just out of his reach. Elisha couldn't help but chuckle.

The smile fell from Elisha's face when she noticed Leena on the dance floor, grinding with Dilawar. They were far too close. She glanced around to see who else was watching her sister drape herself around the young guy. *What the hell was she doing, behaving like she was in a music video at a wedding full of friends, family and not-so-well-wishers?* Elisha stalked up to her.

'Leena! Do you know how you look?' she hissed.

Dilawar immediately disengaged himself, leaving Leena to slump onto her sister.

'You come with me!' Elisha said, holding her wrist, trying to remove her from the dance floor without making a scene.

'*Aaaapa*!' Leena whined. 'We're having so much fun. Don't be a bore.'

'Have you been drinking?' Elisha whispered aghast, catching a whiff of her breath.

'I just took a sip of Dilawar's cranberry juice, I was thirsty. Wanna try some?'

'She grabbed it from me, Elisha, and downed it,' Dilawar said quickly. 'I didn't give it to her. What can I do? She's old enough.'

'She's only sixteen!' Elisha shot him a threatening glance as he walked away.

Leena tried to follow him, pulling Elisha behind her with such force that Elisha felt herself losing her balance.

*Oh God! It will be an utter disaster if we collapse on the dance floor in front of all 800 guests like a pair of drunkards,* Elisha thought in blind panic.

Just then, a strong, steadying hand was thrust forward to help her. It was Faiz. Elisha raised her eyes to silently thank him for sparing her further humiliation and vaguely noticed his mouth was pursed and body had stiffened in disapproval. *He must be shocked at Leena's behaviour, but surely, he's seen worse, and indeed, done worse himself. Typical double standards,* she thought, disappointed. She pulled a reluctant Leena towards her mother who was chatting with Aneela in her customarily loud voice.

'*Dekha*, I told you my girls will do well. That Bhatti boy has been talking to Jahan all night,' she said giggling like a schoolgirl. 'And Faiz Dar has been dancing with Elisha. If I have told them once, I have told them a hundred times, the importance of making a good match. No more tension for me!'

Elisha blushed to the roots of her hair on hearing her mother spouting embarrassing nonsense, instead of keeping an eye on Leena who was young and silly and whose every emotion announced itself on her face. She saw some of the other girls her age drinking and flirting and sought to copy them, not yet understanding that her family wasn't rich or well-connected enough to get away with that sort of behaviour. The Baigs would be torn to shreds by gossipmongers, who, as it is, had a field day with Jameela's utter lack of discretion. It's different when Old Lahore or the children of the very affluent are spotted drinking and dancing, pressed up against some other rich kid – people only criticise who they dare.

She looked around to see who else may have heard her mother and was mortified to see Faiz following her at a discreet distance. He must have heard everything about her mother's purported matchmaking. She knew exactly what he must be thinking, that she'd been a willing part of this plan, that she was like every other girl here. To her immense horror, Elisha realised that embarrassment aside, what Faiz thought of her actually mattered to her.

'Mama, take care of Leena, she's not feeling well,' she said and deposited her burden on to the sofa beside her mother and aunt. 'Maybe we should leave soon?'

'Leave?' her mother said, as if she'd suggested something totally outrageous. 'But the wedding's only really starting now. I saw you dancing earlier with that Faiz Dar, why don't you go and find him again?' her mother said, refraining only from adding a cheeky wink.

'Just keep an eye on Leena, Mama,' Elisha said, sharply, before walking off in search of a sugary cola to fortify herself. The whole evening had been overwhelming so far.

Faiz wove his way through the crowd and found Saif, still engrossed with Jahan.

'Let's go,' Faiz urged his friend.

'Why? I'm having fun. Aren't you enjoying yourself?'

'Not anymore. I saw someone I just can't stand who's ruined my mood.'

Just then there was a momentary lull in the music as the DJ transitioned to more upbeat music, and Faiz's voice carried to where Elisha was standing at the bar behind them. Looking pale and stricken, she assumed that having overheard her mother's remarks and observing her sister's behaviour, Faiz was leaving to get Bhatti away from what he perceived as a totally unsuitable family. When he avoided meeting her eye, she felt sure.

Dinner was announced and the guests started moving towards the tables covered with chafing dishes. Upset, Elisha needed a few minutes alone to clear her head and process her thoughts, so she left the marquee and went inside the empty house to use the loo.

Observing the long line outside the powder room, she ventured further inside the house hoping to find a vacant bathroom.

'Young people nowadays are too much,' an annoyed heavy voice said from the inner recesses of the house. Polly walked up, looking flustered. 'I was looking for a clean bathroom, and I walked into a room with a group bent over the glass table with white powder on it. Dilawar with some boys and a girl also. People have no control over their children. Why would they behave like that and here? So openly. What's the new generation become? Completely rotten!'

Recognising with a sinking heart the flirtatious giggle and excited high-pitched voice coming from the room Polly had pointed out, Elisha waited till the shocked woman had walked away before proceeding towards the room with dread in the pit of her stomach. *No, she wouldn't dare. This was too much.* She tried the door handle, but it had been locked now, some sense had prevailed. But if people were to discover Leena locked in a room full of boys, they would assume the worst, regardless of the truth. She had to get her sister out of there, fast.

'Leena, Leena are you in there?'

'No, she's not here.' It was Dilawar's muffled voice. 'It's just us. Do you wanna join us, Elisha?'

Not giving up, Elisha kept knocking till he, looking annoyed, opened the door a crack and popped his head out to see what was bothering her. She managed to wedge her foot in and spied her youngest sister.

'Leena, what are you doing? Have you lost your mind? You come with me right now! Right now, you hear me!'

'I'm not coming. You can't make me.'

Elisha knew she only had moments before Polly would tell other guests what she had witnessed and they would show up, curious to see whose children were doing drugs, relieved that their own weren't involved. But even with all her weight, she couldn't open the door.

Suddenly, the door was shoved open forcefully and Dilawar reeled back. Faiz strode in, grabbed Leena's hand and led her out of the room. Seeing how upset Elisha looked after she had overheard him, he had followed her to explain himself. Then he had heard the exchange through the door.

'Your sister is waiting for you. I'll deal with you later,' he said grimly, turning in Dilawar's direction.

'Yeah, yeah, we'll see,' Dilawar said, but he looked scared.

'She's not even out of school,' Faiz spat at Dilawar. 'You've screwed up your life, leave her alone.'

'He's my friend. We were just hanging out. I didn't do anything, Elisha, and he didn't force me to come here. I followed him,' Leena tried to play peacemaker and defended her friend, who appeared worldly and glamorous in her eyes.

Dilawar looked at Leena and then looked at Dar and was about to say something but thought better of it. He turned back to the table where the other guys were still huddled around, oblivious to the scene, focused on ensuring none of them should consume too much of the precious substance.

Faiz escorted the two girls out of the house back to the relative safety of the marquee thronged with people.

'I'm sorry, Elisha. You worry for no reason. I wasn't doing anything. I was just talking to those guys. Please don't tell Mama and Papa or they won't let me go out with Dilawar anymore. He's not that bad, just misunderstood,' pleaded Leena. Even their indulgent and somewhat careless parents would have a shit fit at this.

Elisha felt mortified that Faiz had to witness this ignominious scene. Her family had been exposed in front of him in the worst possible light. He probably regretted dancing with her earlier, probably regretted meeting her.

She could only hope to keep Leena out of Polly's sight long enough so she didn't recognise her and recount the story, adding salacious details to spice it up.

Faiz left the girls and purposefully strode off towards Saif who was still engrossed with Jahan.

Saif waved Faiz away, he didn't want his tête-à-tête interrupted. But his determined friend pulled him aside for a private word.

'Come here for a moment,' Dar said firmly. 'You need to find Jahan's father and ask him to take them home. Dilawar's being an asshole as usual. Ask Jahan to call him.'

By then, Elisha had brought her errant young sister to her mother's side and was surprised to see Faiz approaching them. *What could he possibly want with them now?*

'Elisha, I hope you don't mind but I took matters into my own hands. Your father's on his way to take you home. Don't be too angry with your sister. Dilawar's a born troublemaker. I've known him and his family for years. Just seeing him at parties makes me want to leave, he's such bad news. Keep your sister away from him, she's just a kid.'

Astonished, Elisha looked up at him, and smiled gratefully.

'So, I'll see you at tomorrow's event then?' Faiz said.

'Yes, Mr Dar,' Elisha said.

# Begum Saira Returns

## Nida Elley

*"No character, however upright, can escape the malevolence of slander."*

—Lady Susan

As Saira Qadir entered the majestic tented pavilion set up in the front lawn of the Qureishi house, on the grand occasion of their daughter's wedding, she knew that she was being looked at with envy, lust, or resentment. The lust was easily explained.

She wore an electric blue silk sari elegantly draped over a neon-yellow cropped blouse, custom-tailored by a hot young designer called Maheen K. A taupe Kashmiri shawl hung at her elbow, and a forest green Fendi dangled from her wrist. Emerald teardrop earrings hung from her lobes as a matching row of teardrops ran across the delicate tan skin of her neck. Her wavy, shoulder length hair had been blowdried stiff and sat like a dome above her, with sideswept bangs across her forehead. Whatever they were saying about Saira, it would not be that she wasn't au courant. The golden *dori* tying her necklace together at the back of her neck snaked its way down to the middle of her back, where the hem of her sari blouse ended to reveal a sultry slice of flesh just above the waist-level folds of her sari. One might have thought it a bit much for an afternoon wedding, and in any other city it may have been.

Just one year ago, if Saira had made a similar entrance into one of the many social gatherings that took place every week in Lahore, men and women alike would have flocked to her side with hugs, side smooches, covert winks, and welcoming smiles. But today, on the first day of 1989, everything was different. She actually felt nervous making an entrance. She'd been dressing to the nines and attending parties since her own wedding twenty-two years ago. Her mother had been a great and gracious beauty, a fact she was only too aware of. Her younger sister hadn't taken her looks. And so as a girl, all her mother's hopes had ridden on Saira. She'd been painstakingly instructed on how to dress for various occasions, how to host a party, how to make the perfect cup of tea, and how to mask disinterest and converse with people she didn't especially want to speak to. It was the period of exile leading up to this evening that made it feel rather like her first night out. And the fact that previously she'd always been accompanied by her late husband, Iqbal Rashid Qadir. His senior role at the bank had required them to attend a stream of social functions. Though he would have been much happier sitting in his study with a book, he realized the significant career benefit of being social, and more importantly, how much it thrilled his young wife. He'd have done anything for her, and it's true, she had enjoyed being the belle of the ball. No one had been prepared for Iqbal to suddenly die of a massive heart attack at the age of forty-nine. Along with feeling his loss, she felt something else, she just couldn't put her finger on it.

*We have a woman prime minister*, Saira thought, trying to look confident weaving her way through the scattered pots of burning coal warming the brisk January air inside the marquee. *We have a woman prime minister, I can attend a wedding on my own*, she repeated to herself. So much had changed in this last year, she'd been so taken up with the upheaval in her own life that she was only just absorbing it.

In August, President Zia had been killed in a plane crash; just a month ago, Benazir Bhutto had become the first female head of state of Pakistan, indeed, of any Islamic nation. The country felt alive with hope after a very long time. Saira guiltily felt touched by it even in her period of mourning. She'd never attended any of the protests against Zia; Iqbal's family didn't like that sort of thing. But her college friend Shahmeen was a journalist and very involved. When Shahmeen came to visit her last, she looked jubilant, sparkly with hope. She said more than anything she wanted the women-hating *mullahs* who'd protested Benazir's win to finally sod off and bury themselves in the ground besides Zia's grave. She hoped the country would reverse its backward trek into the dark ages, and take its place among the progressive nations of the world. *It was hard to tell*, Saira thought, looking around, *if anything had moved forward or not.*

She glided in the general direction of the main stage where the bride and groom sat. Heavily jewelled and made-up, the bride was anchored to her sofa by the sheer weight of her burnished bridal gown, covered as it was in traditionally embroidered *dabka* and edged with golden *gota*. The groom sat beside her with a goofy-looking smile, most likely, Saira thought, happy in the knowledge that he would never have to spend a sexless night on his own again. But she was not there to meet the couple just yet.

'Tehmina, there you are!' she said, greeting the mother of the bride, with the enthusiasm of seeing a long-lost friend. 'I was looking all over for you. But, oh my, how stunning you look!' She took a step back, looking her up and down, trying to look sincere in her admiration of Tehmina's ridiculously full-skirted scarlet *gharara*. Typically, red was reserved for the bride, but, Saira thought, not today. 'What a vision you are! You look like Tania's older sister, much less her mother.'

Tehmina chuckled at Saira's praise with delight. 'Oh, Saira! Stop! You're embarrassing me. It's so good to see you. I'm so glad you could make it.'

'How could I not? I still can't believe Tania is getting married. It seems like it was just yesterday when she and my Masooma were playing with their Barbies and putting on fashion shows in our heels and saris.' Saira's expression softened as she thought of her daughter, Masooma, who was at college in the States.

'I can't believe it myself,' Tehmina said, as she held Saira's hands in both of hers and gently squeezed them. Spotting someone and jerking her head abruptly to the side, Tehmina begged leave to continue with her duties as hostess, 'I'm so sorry, *haan*, I just have to check something. Do mingle and enjoy yourself. I'm really just thrilled you came.' Her voice trailed off as she held up both sides of her voluminous *gharara* and tottered away on rickety heels. Saira watched her walking towards the buffet tables that were still being set up for lunch, barking orders at the waiters, who were all dressed in brick-colored *shalwar kameezes*. Some of them were skewering *seekh kababs* and *chicken botis* over a makeshift grill. Others brought out steaming silver dishes of lamb *biryani* and spinach *paneer*, while others moved jangling crates of Coke, Sprite, and Fanta glass bottles from the catering truck to the drinks table. Qureishi *saab*, who was himself, at that moment, taking stock of the lunch situation, walked up beside his wife and discreetly whispered something into her ear. Then he glanced back at Saira with a weak smile.

It seemed that ever since Iqbal had died, many of their society friends had collectively decided to shun her, while still publicly promising to be there if she needed them. She knew how hypocrisy worked, but it still hurt when someone you'd invited to your home every second week for twenty-two years, someone whose children had grown up with yours, looked as if they wished you weren't there. And Farooq Qureishi, who'd once walked her to a secluded nook of his garden during a dinner party and shot her yearning looks till he heard the voices of other guests nearby.

A few years into Saira and Iqbal's marriage, it had become clear that the wives of most of his friends and colleagues didn't like her. She was vibrant and sexy, and she enoyed attention, none of which did her any favours in her social set. One night, at a dinner party at the Awans, Saira had been telling a story about her and Iqbal's recent trip to London.

'We had the most wonderful time,' she'd said, swaying at the memory. It was the early 1970s and short shirts with fitted waists and loose *shalwars* were in fashion. Her tea pink shirt silhouetted her generous curves, while her sheer *dupatta* was tugged back against her neck, more a fashion accessory than an attempt at modesty. 'We were staying with Iqbal's younger cousin, Monty, who's studying to be a chartered accountant. Now Monty, you must know, has decided not only to look the part of a Brit, but to sound the part, as well. So one night he asked us, in his heavily put-on British accent, whether we wanted to go to a "paahty". Of course, silly girl that I am, I thought he was asking us if we needed to do potty.' Some of the women giggled nervously while others backed away in disgust. This only made more room for more men to crowd around her and enjoy the show. 'You see, he only had one bathroom in his flat, and if someone else needed to use it, they would have to run across the street to the petrol station. So I thought it was his way of asking us if we wanted to *go* before he went ahead and did so himself.'

The men laughed uproariously. She used her whole body to talk, exuding a charismatic energy. As the night wore on and she continued to hog the spotlight, some of the guests started to find her unbearable. *Who does she think she is? Just because she's young and pretty, she can get away with telling crass stories and making herself the centre of attention?*

Rumours started circulating that the young bride was being too flirtatious with some of the other women's husbands. Of course, nobody ever blamed the men, Saira thought, nor considered them capable of initiating these flirtations. Over time, Saira developed a reputation for being a little too candid. The rumours never found their way to Iqbal's ears, but Saira always knew exactly what people said about her. The sniping didn't bother her because Iqbal's boundless love was her buffer against the lot of them. It had been such a heady feeling, living with a man who worshipped the ground she walked on, who spared no expense in making her happy, with the end result that now she had less of his savings to sustain herself than expected. It was a life Saira easily became accustomed to, and even though she never truly felt that she was *in love* with him, she loved him simply for being so good to her. Of course they said she'd 'stolen' him, as if he were an object to pickpocket with no will of his own. Iqbal had first been engaged to Saira's older cousin, Sabrina, but while visiting his fiancée, he saw Saira and told his parents later that day that if he were to be married, it would be to her and her alone.

Saira had kept a low profile all year. It was no hardship; she hadn't been in the mood to attend lunches and parties without Iqbal. She had mourned his departure with the requisite humility expected of a widow, and she missed her friend, but now that a year had passed, she felt ready to move on. After all, she was only forty.

'Darling! Over here! I'm over here!' chirped a bulky woman with a short feathery crop inspired by Princess Di, dressed head to toe in gold organza.

'Nina, thank God!' Nina was her closest confidante. In a world of conformist phonies, Nina was exactly who she was, which was warm, honest, and blissfully without a sense of fashion. 'What are you doing?' she asked as Nina took her by the arm and steered her towards a corner where they could sit on a plush sofa and speak privately.

'I just have to tell you…I saw the craziest thing. In fact, it's so crazy, I'm not quite sure it really happened, but then, why would I be hallucinating? I have perfect 20/20 vision.' Nina's hands weighed down by ornate rings of all shapes and sizes, gesticulated wildly as she spoke.

'Nina, calm down, what happened?'

'I,' she paused emphatically, 'just saw Fakirullah Jahan, Mr Holier Than Thou himself, brush his hands against Samina Jatoi's. It was *not* accidental. Can you imagine? After all the trash she said about you last week at her grandson's *aqiqa*. Behaving as if you were Alexis from *Dynasty*, wanting to steal her husband. As if you would even entertain the idea of that crude, pot-bellied, balding man...she, of all people, brushed her hands against his and, I tell you, Saira, I tell you with 100% certainty, they exchanged a knowing look!' she said, looking around to see if anyone had overheard her. 'Uff, I can't stand this place, and if I had half a chance, I'd move to the States and start life afresh with some bloody dignity. Which is what you should be doing!'

'I told you,' Saira said, 'I told you there was something fishy going on there and you just didn't believe me. But I knew. I knew it as soon as I bumped into both her and Fakirullah on the same day, at the same hotel. Anyway,' she waved her hand in the air, dismissing the subject. 'I don't give a damn about these people and their little affairs. They can do whatever they damn well please. It's really none of my business. But to turn around and then malign me? And for *what*? Because their sleazy husbands can't keep their wandering eyes to themselves? What have I done, other than keep to myself this past year, and think only of my darling daughter and seeing her settle down?'

'How is Masooma?'

'She's loving the States', Saira said. 'I wish she didn't like it so much. I miss her. She rang the other day to ask if I'd mail her a Vital Signs cassette. She heard a song at one of her Pakistani friend's houses there and she thinks they sound great!' she added, laughing.

'That Junaid Jamshed is so cute,' Nina said, giggling. 'Our kids will have it better than we did, Saira. See how young people are doing things in Pakistan? Now Zia's gone, things can only get better. Though you know what they're saying about Benazir. That she's married that slimy Zardari and that'll be the end of her. I hope not.'

Saira and Nina sat back on the sofa. Saira's eyes scanned the room. The men wore either designer suits or starched white *kurtas* with fitted black waistcoats, and grouped together in vigorous debate. The women were swathed in vibrant saris and *shalwar kameez*, bedecked with shimmering jewels and extravagant hairdos that smelled pungently of Aqua Net hairspray, mingled with Calvin Klein's Obsession. Several guests held wineglasses filled with orange and pomegranate juice, no doubt spiked with a little something from the hidden backstage bar. There was an assortment of savoury hors d'eouvres going around; one woman was struggling to eat a flaky vol-au-vent without cutting a swathe through her glossy burgundy lipstick.

'Those *samosas* look good' Nina said.

'Shall I get us some? You keep my seat.' Saira rose and headed towards the crowd. Now that she was looking, there wasn't a waiter in sight.

'Look at her, wearing that loud outfit, baring all that skin, strutting around like Madonna,' she heard from within a knot of people. The voice was so familiar, she stopped to listen.

'I actually think she's quite attractive,' said another voice, one she'd not heard before.

'You're new here, *na*, you don't know. If being married didn't stop her from flirting with everyone's husband, being widowed definitely won't.'

Saira flushed and backed away, though not so far that she couldn't continue to eavesdrop.

'Did she ever…?' asked the other lady, incredulous.

'That I don't know.' Saira figured out whose voice it was. Her older cousin, Sabrina. The one Iqbal had been due to marry. 'But who knows what a woman who can turn on her own relatives is capable of.'

'What do you mean?'

'Oh, that's a story for another time. Come, let me introduce you to Tammy Khan. If you know her, it's like knowing everyone in town.' The voices faded as the women walked away.

After all these years, despite being married with three children of her own, Sabrina still couldn't get over what she saw as Saira's betrayal. She'd given her the cold shoulder at family functions and chimed in, Saira knew, with everyone who'd ever cast aspersions on her through the years. They were all floating about here somewhere, she thought, as she stepped out of the crowd to catch her breath.

And yet, she thought, in spite of it all, there was something she loved about Lahore. It was the city of her birth, of lazy childhood days dancing in the monsoon rain, and sweaty days cursing the summer heat. It was the city where she'd been wed, where her daughter had been born. Where she could always find ways and means of getting what she wanted, either openly or discreetly, through a network of friends, relatives, maids, drivers, and so on. It was a city where the men in the bazaar would either stare at her lasciviously trying their best to brush their hands against her rear, or else lower their eyes and treat her with the utmost respect. It was where the wives of her husband's colleagues would praise her almond-shaped eyes, her long lashes and the dimple on her smiling cheek, while simultaneously spreading vile rumors about her. Lahore was a city of contradictions and extremes. Nina had, for a long time, been pushing her to move, to make a fresh start in a new city where she wouldn't be weighed down by everyone's judgement, but Saira knew, without a doubt, her life wouldn't be as exciting anywhere else. She couldn't imagine living in some isolated rural suburb in the West with nothing to entertain her. It was excitement she had always craved, that feeling of being desired or despised, but with a passion. She felt she would rather die than live without passion.

She returned to Nina on the sofa.

'Couldn't find the *samosas*, sorry' she said.

'Never mind that, darling! Look over there, by that large bouquet of tuberoses, it's your little sister and her boyfriend. Her fiancé, right?' Nina's eyes glittered with mischief. 'Does she know that Ghalib once had eyes only for you? That he practically proposed to you every day in college?'

'Oh, Nina, how could you even say that? That's all in the past. Shahana only needs to know that now Ghalib loves her and only her.' Saira glanced over at her sister, trying to catch her eye. A stranger wouldn't have known Shahana was Saira's sister. Where Saira had taken her mother's fine features with her high cheekbones and dimples, Shahana had a solid, homelier aspect and lacked Saira's quick wit. Still, she looked very pretty today, Saira thought, with a fresh perm, in an oversized red cardigan with shoulder pads over a cheetah print *kameez*. What Nina had said was true. But what Saira had never told her, or indeed anyone, was that she'd actually been tempted to marry Ghalib before Iqbal – a much safer bet – had shown up. She couldn't imagine how angry Shahana would feel if she found out. 'Now, don't say anything inappropriate in front of them. My sister is quite in love with this one. They've been together for more than a year, although, rascal that he is, he keeps delaying when she suggests a date.' She waved at Shahana and Ghalib till they saw her and began to walk over.

'I'm telling you,' said Nina. 'There's something I don't trust about that man. You told me yourself, he was Mr. Casanova in college. Ooh, excuse me darling, I have to say hello to Saeeda! SAEEDA!' she shouted in the direction of a woman walking in, speeding in her direction.

Ghalib and Shahana joined Saira at the sofa. The two sisters hugged and kissed. Ghalib warmly, and rather unexpectedly, embraced her. 'How are things, Ghalib?' she said. 'And how are Mama and Papa?' she asked Shahana.

'The usual,' Shahana said, rolling her eyes. 'Always talking about you, wondering when you'll come to visit, thinking of potential matches for Masooma.' As Shahana bent down to sit, one of her heels got stuck in the threads of the carpet beneath them, and she stumbled. Bent over at an awkward angle, she attempted to unwind the threads from her thin heel. Saira noticed that Ghalib didn't even offer to help her.

'Sit, Shahana,' she said. 'Let me help you,' Saira said, freeing her sister's shoe.

'If only our parents had spent this much time thinking about me, I wouldn't be such an old maid now.' Shahana laughed away the remark, but Saira knew she meant it. Five years Saira's junior, Shahana felt like she had grown up in the shadow of her glamorous older sister. She'd resented her when every relationship of hers had fallen through in the past. She felt like she'd spent half her life chasing men, while Saira just had to sit back and look disinterested and they all came running.

She looked over at Ghalib and smiled. 'Well, hopefully not for too long.'

Ghalib ignored the pointed comment. 'You're a vision, today, Saira. And it's good to see you out again.' His eyes glossed over her outfit, spending a fraction of a second too long taking in the view of her exposed waistline. 'I still remember the first time I saw you all dressed up with powdered skin and blush. It was on the night of the Annual Play at Government College. Do you remember?'

'Oh, Ghalib,' Saira said, laughing. 'Why are you reminding me of our college days? That was eons ago. In fact, it's been more than twenty years.' She remembered how his handsome face and wry humour had made the girls swoon. She'd not been totally immune herself but she'd acted as if none of that had any effect on her. And anyway, she was betrothed to Iqbal two years later, leaving college before completing her degree.

'Apa,' Shahana said, feeling left out. 'Are those grey hairs I see? Have you stopped dyeing?'

Saira glared at her, and she smirked.

'When are you going to come visit? Mama and Papa are always worrying about how you're all alone in that house.'

It was true. Saira lived on her own now, with just a couple of servants for company. Her mother-in-law had died a few years ago, then Masooma had left for college. Without Iqbal to talk to, she often felt like a shadow floating from one room to the other.

'I'll come on the weekend as always, Shahana. I've just been busy trying to redecorate.' Sometimes she pretended it was a brand new house that she'd just moved into. As if it were a new life. 'You both must come visit me soon and see all the changes.'

'Where is the house again?' Ghalib asked. 'On Gulberg Main Boulevard? I think Shahana pointed it out once when we were driving past. It's the one with the bright green gate, right?' Saira nodded. He stood up. 'Would you excuse me, I have to find a few friends here. See you both later.' He gave Shahana's shoulder a squeeze, and looked at Saira as if he was about to say something but then thought better of it.

'I really wish Mama and Papa wouldn't worry about me. I mean, I'm forty years old, for God's sake. I've spent half my life taking care of my own family', Saira said to Shahana, who rolled her eyes again. It was a most unbecoming gesture. 'Now tell me' she said, 'how are things really going with Ghalib?'

'What exactly do you mean?'

'Oh, please, Shahana. I've known him far longer than you. I know what he can be like. Especially when it comes to women. Not for nothing has he never married. Have you two set a date yet?'

'In fact,' Shahana said in hushed tones, 'we've finally decided to get married in October. Ghalib doesn't want me to tell anyone yet. Now we just have to decide which weekend.' She beamed like a little girl who had just been handed a prize. 'Isn't that wonderful?'

Saira sighed. 'Well, yes, of course. That's great.' She didn't sound convinced.

'How is Masooma? Can we expect to see her soon? I hope she'll be here for the wedding.'

'She's graduating in May, but just the other day she said she wanted to stay on in America for a bit to see if she could look for job opportunities. What kind of a mother would I be if I told her not to? But I can't imagine living so far away from her. I was thinking maybe if she had some incentive to stay, she'd forget all about the US.' She looked at Shahana with a mischievous grin.

'*Aapa*, what exactly are you planning?' Shahana asked, accusingly.

'Well, I haven't found a *rishta* just yet. But I do have someone in mind.' Saira surveyed the crowd, which had mostly moved in the direction of the food.

Eventually, the sisters proceeded to the the buffet table where they were split up by people squeezing between them, displaying the customary Pakistani reluctance to queue. Saira ladled a small serving of chicken *biryani* onto her plate, looking around to see if she could spot someone she might want to sit with. Saira saw Nina waving wildly to her from afar, but she didn't relish the thought of having forced conversation with her husband. He wasn't sleazy like other Lahori men but he was dull, which wasn't all that much better. Where, oh where, was Azaad Kamaal, the 30-year-old heir to Kamaal Industries? Saira had heard rumours that his parents were looking for a potential wife for him. Iqbal and Saira had been well-acquainted with his parents, often invited to lavish dinner parties at their ancestral *haveli*. She felt, perhaps, that she had a slight upper hand. Well, it wasn't just that, of course. She had got to know him a little more intimately than she'd wanted.

A 19-year-old Azaad had once found her standing alone on one of the many terraces of his house, annoyed. She'd just fielded one of Tammy Khan's snide remarks, 'How lovely that Iqbal *bhai* isn't one of those jealous cave men types. Most Lahori men blow a fuse if a woman so much as says hello to another man! Iqbal *bhai* is so evolved.' Saira's lips had pulled into a thin smile at essentially being called a slut, albeit not directly, and instead of letting the cow think she'd touched a nerve by losing her cool, she'd excused herself for a breath of fresh air.

When Azaad found her, she'd been standing there in another one of her silk *Banarsi* saris, having a cigarette and resting her free arm on the terrace railing.

'How come you aren't downstairs, enjoying the party, Auntie?'

Saira nearly choked on the smoke. She was little more than a decade older than him. 'Auntie? Please, darling. Do me the favour of not making me feel so old. Just call me Saira. And as to your question, well...there are certain people I wish had never been born. Except they were. And they're at this party.

So I'm giving myself a little time-out to recoup.' She offered him a cigarette. He was a little shocked, but took one. 'Now, your turn. How come you're not at the party? Your parents must have asked you to make an appearance, now that you're a college boy, visiting from England and all.'

Azaad scoffed. 'Yeah, more like, they instructed me to attend.' He looked out into the starless night with a sneer.

'Everything okay?' Saira asked. She turned to face him. 'Really. I'm very good at keeping secrets, and even better at giving advice,' she said, followed by a conspiratorial wink.

'Thank you. That's really kind. But I'm fine, really. I'm just not in the mood for people, you know.' He took a long drag on his cigarette. 'My dad's very big on that, getting me to know people who matter.'

'I'm sure he is,' Saira said. 'But I'm guessing you're more interested in having fun. A dinner party full of stuffy old people probably pales in comparison to all the other, more exciting things you could be doing.'

'Well, firstly, not everyone here tonight is old and stuffy. I can name at least one person who's pretty interesting.' He smiled.

'Flattery will get you nowhere, darling,' she said laughing, till he reached forward and held her hand.

'I think I'm right where I want to be.'

Saira blushed, immediately realising that she'd been too open, too casual with him.

She laughed nervously, while extricating her hand from his. 'Aren't you just a sweetheart! Trying to make your Auntie feel young again.' She put the cigarette out on the railing and left it there. 'You know, I probably should be getting back to the party. Before Iqbal sends out a search team for me.' She put her hand on his shoulder, in as maternal a way as she could manage. 'It was so nice to see you. All dashing and grown up.' She began to walk back inside.

'You know, you didn't have to do that,' he smirked.

She turned halfway around. 'What?' she asked, innocently.

He walked towards her, with his jaw clenched. For a moment, Saira thought he might hit her. But instead, he tenderly placed one hand on her cheek, and the other on her hip, pulling her close enough to him that she could feel his warm, whisky breath on her face. 'I'm not as young as you think, you know. And I'm sure we could have a much better time if we both ditched this party.'

Panicked, she pushed him away and fled to the nearest staircase. Her pulse raced as she scurried downstairs and into a bathroom before anyone could see her. Locking the door, she took a deep breath and just stared at herself in the mirror. *How strange*, she thought. That hadn't gone at all as expected. At first, she giggled like a schoolgirl and then started scolding herself. Why would he say such a thing? She didn't know what bothered her more – the fact that he'd hit on her, or the fact that it gave her such a thrill.

She re-joined the party that night, but every time she saw Azaad thereafter, he'd make a point of getting her attention. Sometimes he'd wink at her from afar, or brush his hand against hers. Once he even whispered in her ear when no one was watching, 'Looking hot, Saira.' Each time she'd get that flip-flop feeling in her stomach, and then curse herself for being so silly. The only time she'd known him to be restrained had been the last time she had seen him, at Iqbal's funeral.

Now, as she continued to scan the wedding guests, holding her plate and taking small bites, she felt a tap on her shoulder.

'Looking for me?' And there he was. She quickly dabbed the corners of her lips with a napkin and turned to face him. 'It's nice to see you, Saira.' He was wearing a well-tailored suit with a white, button down shirt and a black bowtie. He had a blue and green checked handkerchief peeking out of his chest pocket and his hands tucked away in his pants' pockets in an irritatingly self-assured way. 'It's been a while,' he said.

'Y-yes, yes, it has,' she stuttered, coughing away her sudden nervousness. 'How are you, Azaad? I had heard from your parents that you were in town and already taking over the family business. How does it feel to be back?' She leaned towards the nearest buffet table and placed her uneaten lunch there. She had suddenly lost her appetite.

'That's right, I'm back. I got tired of living abroad and working like a dog for the Man. That life just wasn't for me.' He took his hands out of his pockets and crossed them over his chest. She wasn't getting any flirtatious vibes from him at all. 'Plus, it was getting lonely. And my parents were pressuring me to come back. So I just bit the bullet, quit my job, and packed up.'

Saira knew it was crazy to have had the tingles from the same man she wanted for a son-in-law. But she knew Azaad would give Masooma a comfortable life. He'd keep her in Lahore. And, perhaps, she hoped, he'd exhibit the same passion towards her daughter that he'd once shown her. Masooma, she thought, was smarter and kinder and more sensitive than Saira had ever been and Saira hoped she would get to experience love, not just marriage.

'So how are you finding it here?' she asked.

He seemed to consider that question for a while. 'I'm not sure. It's definitely a transition. My family are pretty in-your-face. I'm trying to get used to the intrusiveness, not to mention the constant discussions about the servants. Don't even get me started on the load shedding.'

'You know, I'm worried about the very same thing for my daughter. Masooma…remember her? She's studying at Columbia right now, but she'll be graduating this summer, and hopefully, returning home. I'm sure it'll be tough on her, too.'

'I'm sure it will.'

'Perhaps you could meet for coffee when she's back and give her some tips on how to make the adjustment.'

'Sure. I'd love to meet her. It's been a while. I think the last time I saw her was when she was nine. Wow, I can't believe it's been twelve years since then.'

He touched Saira's arm gently. 'How are you doing?'

'I'm all right, thank you. It's been a tough year but...I'm a survivor.' She smiled.

'Yes, you are, aren't you?'

After an awkward pause, Saira tried to cheerfully retreat. 'Well, it's been so lovely to see you. You must come visit us, when Masooma is back.'

'Of course,' he said, hugging her warmly and without impropriety. She walked over to join the hordes of well-wishers who had started to gather round the bride and groom for pictures. Thank God, he hadn't made any reference to their past exchanges. At that instant, it felt to Saira as if nothing of any consequence had transpired between her and Azaad. Maybe she had dreamed it all up in her head.

She thought about getting in line for a picture with the bride and groom. She thought about saying goodbye to the Qureishis, or checking in with Nina or Shahana. But she didn't do any of those things. She swerved back in the direction of the entrance and walked out of the marquee.

Saira was driven home by her part-time driver who she excused for the rest of the day. She had a part-time cook and cleaning lady as well, but they too had gone home. Saira relished the thought of an empty house; all she wanted was to get out of her heels and crawl into her bed for a late afternoon nap. Or perhaps, a cup of hot tea first. *Yes*, she thought. *A cup of tea would be perfect on this chilly day*.

She let herself into the hallway, which led to a dining room on one side and a kitchen on the other, and opened up into a formal living room at the opposite end, and then a smaller, more intimate family room where she kicked off her heels. She walked barefoot towards the middle of living room. Closing the doors that separated the living room from the hall and the family room, she turned on the gas heater and sat in front of it till she felt the room warm up around her. Saira felt the heat melt away her tension, felt her muscles relaxing. In that moment, she felt possessed by a delicious sense of freedom with all her staff away, her parents in their own home, her husband gone.

Overcome by a feeling of lightness, she began to turn slowly, unspooling herself out of her sari. She let it fall in gauzy layers at her feet, and stepped over the silken sprawl in just her blouse, with its plunging neckline, and her petticoat. It had warmed up enough for her to roam about like this.

Saira stood for a while, walking around the room, trying to imagine where to place her new furniture once it arrived, and where to hang her paintings. The thought of not having to ask somebody else's opinion on redecorating felt like a strange sort of new pleasure. She would convert the house from being her husband's home to her own, a reflection of her adult self and all the changes she'd gone through in this last year. She wanted the place to look rich with works of art and foliage, not dourly lined with black and white family portraits of three generations of the Qadir family.

She knew decorating it at all was reckless; apart from this house, her inheritance included Iqbal's limited assets and a small pension. She'd probably have to sell the house but she didn't want to think about that now. The alternative was thinking of ways to earn an income, with an unfinished college degree.

The sound of the doorbell disrupted her thoughts. She wasn't expecting any visitors. Irritated, she grabbed her shawl from the sofa and wrapped it around her shoulders and chest. Upon opening the door, she was astonished to discover Ghalib, tipsy and teetering a little on his feet.

'Ghalib? What are you doing here? Is Shahana here, too?' she asked, looking over his shoulder for her sister.

'No, I just dropped her home,' he said. 'I needed to see you. To talk to you.' He took a few steps inside, and then stood awkwardly in the middle of the hallway, looking out of place. She wondered what he could possibly want.

'Is everything okay, Ghalib? Is this about Shahana? Please tell me that she is right in assuming there will be a wedding in October.'

'We need to talk about it, Saira.'

Saira led the way to the living room and gestured for him to sit down. He look puzzled at the sight of her sari strewn on the living room floor, but said nothing.

'Well?' she asked, still standing. 'Out with it, Ghalib.'

He cradled his head in his hands and said, 'I can't do it, Saira. I can't marry her.'

Saira waited for the shock of those words to hit her, but it never quite came. She supposed she had been expecting this very moment, ever since the pair had got together. She knew Ghalib couldn't be trusted. He had always been both flirtatious and vain, even when they were in college. This had been why, in spite of being tempted, she'd never responded to his attentions. She sighed and sat down at the opposite end of the sofa.

'It's not what you're thinking,' he said.

'How could you possibly know what I'm thinking?'

'I know you, Saira. I'm aware of the fact that you don't trust me. But you must also be aware of the fact that I love you. I loved you when we were in college, and I love you now. It has always been you that I wanted. And now that you're...well...alone, I thought perhaps...' He looked at her with such earnestness, she almost felt bad for him.

'You thought perhaps what?' she asked, coldly. 'That I would gladly betray my one and only sister and walk off into the sunset with you? That I'd forget the fact that you are the scum of the earth and so beneath me and my sister, that I'd throw away my integrity and self-respect to be with you?' She jumped to her feet and walked through the adjoining family room, towards her bedroom door. 'Just go, Ghalib. What are you doing here? Leave before I say something I'll regret.' She strode into her dark bedroom and slammed the door behind her, boiling from within. She snatched the first thing she saw – her pillow – and started thrashing it against her bed. What did he think of himself? Her sister would be heartbroken. And her parents! First the death of their son-in-law, then the broken engagement of their daughter – what further tragedy would they have to endure?

She soon tired of expending her anger onto the pillow. She slumped onto the corner of her bed.

She heard a gentle knock on the door. 'Saira,' he said. 'I'm leaving. I just wanted to apologize. Please, open the door, and let me explain. I didn't mean to upset you.' His voice was timid, slightly slurring. *He's drunk*, she thought. *That's why he is saying all this nonsense. He's just drunk*.

'Saira, please,' he said, pleading. 'I never meant for things to turn out this way. I wasn't thinking of it so much as a betrayal of Shahana. I guess, I was thinking of it more as an opportunity. For you and me. A fresh start. Something I'd dreamt of years ago. I thought it might still be possible.'

He grew silent for a few minutes. 'Okay,' he said. 'I'll go. Just please know, I'm sorry.'

'Wait,' she said, opening the door. 'Just wait.'

He turned back and looked at her. She walked past him, back into the hallway, and through a swinging door on one side that led to the kitchen. He followed her there. She filled the kettle with water and placed it on the stove. Then she lit the flame beneath it, and reached for two mugs from the cupboard to her right. She opened the canister of tea leaves and placed a spoon at the ready. The ritual calmed her down.

Turning around, leaning against the kitchen counter, she said, 'You caught me off guard, Ghalib. I need time to process what you're saying. Let's just cool down and have a cup of tea. Then we can talk.'

She gave him an awkward smile, then turned back to making the tea. As she stood there, with her back to Ghalib, she could feel him move closer. His arms wrapped around her waist from behind as he slid one side of her shawl to the side and began to kiss the sensitive skin between her neck and shoulder. Her eyelids closed momentarily in unexpected pleasure, but then she pushed his cheek away and told him to go sit.

'I said we can talk, Ghalib. Nothing else.' He looked sheepish, then turned towards the living room. He would sit and wait for her, and hopefully sober up.

Her breathing had quickened; her face had flushed, too. She could still feel tingles in different parts of her body. It had been a while since someone had touched her that way. She took a deep breath and allowed herself to think for a moment about her and Ghalib. She didn't dislike him. He'd always been charming and sweet, when sober.

She couldn't deny the fact that it would be nice to have someone love her again, to pamper her, and listen to her, and keep her warm at night.

She felt a stab of guilt in her gut for even thinking this way. Poor Shahana! If Saira took this step, her sister would most likely cut herself off from Saira altogether. Despite their differences, she loved Shahana deeply. But the reality of the situation was that Ghalib was likely to leave her no matter what. Whether he disappeared or entered into a new relationship, he and Shahana were over. So why couldn't her sister's misfortune be an opportunity for someone else?

Saira was the victim of so much misfortune herself, with Iqbal gone, and their former friends ostracising her. Her own daughter wanted to abandon her. If Masooma married Azaad, Saira would never have to worry about her daughter anymore; she would consider her motherly responsibilities over and could start her life afresh.

The thought was so pleasing that she unconsciously smiled to herself as she spooned tea leaves into the ceramic teapot and added water. Setting it onto a tray with matching cups and milk and sugar, she carried it into the living room. Bending down to place it on the coffee table, one end of her shawl fell off her shoulder, revealing a glimpse of cleavage. Hurriedly, she picked up the shawl to cover herself, but she saw in Ghalib's eye a look which confirmed to her that her sister was the furthest thing from his mind. She poured milk and added sugar to his cup, before placing it in his hands. Their fingers briefly touched and she experienced that tingly sensation all over again.

Taking her own mug, she sat down next to him. 'Okay' Saira said, taking a deep breath. 'Let's talk.'

# Emaan Ever After

**Mishayl Naek**

*"If I loved you less, I might be able to talk about it more"*

—Emma

Not only am I dressed and out at half past eight, I'm in fashion sportswear. I'd bought it to encourage myself to go to the gym, which is where I'd actually been headed this morning, before deciding to stop for a power smoothie at my favourite bistro first. Well, one thing led to another, and now I appear to have ordered a rather large breakfast and scrapped the idea of the gym. I love Xanders with its grass green and slate grey interior but I'm unused to being here this early, and find myself surrounded by Karachi's top one per cent nibbling at their egg-white omelettes and granola bowls with imported berries. I've slunk into a booth with my iPad, partly because since I'm here, I may as well get some work done, and partly because I'm not sure I have the courage to be seen wolfing down scrambled eggs, with yolks, and a fair amount of butter, by women emaciated to the point of not getting their period any longer.

And speaking of emaciated women, I'm flicking through pictures from a recent society wedding that I have to caption. Working at Panache comes with its perks—FROW at seemingly endless local fashion weeks—but having to deal with the hysteria of designers whose clothes didn't make the cut is undoing the effects of my recent (super-secret) Botox. Being thirty-two and divorced in Karachi society requires your dermatologist and personal trainer on speed dial. Don't judge—the competition is twenty-two. Not that I'm dying to remarry, mind you. Far from it. My friends tell me, kindly, I fear, that I have pretty almond eyes, a rosebud mouth and that I go in and out in all the right places. But all you think about standing next to some sort of twenty-nothing Barbie at a party is how you wish you could go back in time and make better decisions regarding carbohydrate intake.

I've made a lot of questionable decisions over the years if I'm honest. Although I did Economics at the LSE, I've somehow ended up becoming the deputy editor of a lifestyle magazine in Karachi. I gave the banking sector a shot in London after uni. More than a shot. I did it for seven miserable years before realising that if I hadn't failed, I hadn't exactly succeeded either. Bless my Punjabi papa and his unfailing humour! My mother passed away when I was a baby, and being an only child, I have definitely tested his patience. Along with the Economics degree ending in a job that wouldn't cover my bills if I actually had to pay them myself, there was the princess-level wedding followed by a divorce. I feel the change in career was more upsetting to my ambitious father than my divorce – he owns textile mills he hadn't inherited, and growing up, while all the Aunties were trying to get me married off, he was all about my education.

If he hates what I do, he hasn't said anything. My father isn't the most expressive person, but I know he understands how much I needed the change of scene when I returned to Karachi to rebuild my life after my divorce. I came back confused and hurt – even though marriage hadn't been wonderful – and filling up my days with TV and listless shopping trips was making me even more miserable. A school-friend whose father owns a publishing house offered me this job as a lifeline. Admittedly much of my work involved coming up with different ways of saying 'socialite', but I'd be lying if I said I didn't enjoy it. I'd been at it for a year and along with editing copy, I was writing things for the first time. The thrill of seeing my byline alongside my pieces, sometimes being shared on social media, hadn't got at all old. The only thing getting old, as I was saying earlier, was me.

I chew on my bottom lip and think about dinner later this evening. A school-friend and her husband are having dinner and drinks for twenty at their place. Both bankers, they spend a great deal of time travelling and don't entertain often, so I don't know beforehand – as with most Karachi gatherings – who to expect. I allow my mind to flirt with the possibility of an interesting single male, though I know the chances are slim, even slimmer than the girls who'll be lining up to bag him if he exists. Men at these things are usually aged, often crass, and typically pickled in whiskey. What is about Pakistani men that allow them to be hideous, both in looks and in nature?

As if to prove the exception to the rule, my WhatsApp pings with a message from the only single man I know who isn't a complete troll. He's also the last man I'd get involved with, so he doesn't count anyway.

**Haroon**
*Stop obsessing over how you're looking. Are you going to this dinner tonight?*

**Emaan**
*Are you reading my mind now?! Yesssss I think so. Are you?*

**Haroon**
*I am now. See you tonight. Wear something skimpy so I can tell your father. Ta.*

I fork up some more scrambled egg, smiling. He's such an idiot. I check my phone to see if I can waste some more time on social media and am rewarded with ample opportunity. I spot a hashtag for a charity brunch, where, from what I can see, everyone was excruciatingly badly dressed. They're wearing hats as if they're at Ascot! I feel better.

I snuck into an evening Spin class at Studio X, and now I'm lying on my bed in sweaty gym clothes, ruminating over how my lady bits are numb from the bike seat and how that's probably the most action they're going to get this year. It's only a few months away from the December wedding season and I wonder, not for the first time, how people are continuing to pair up and get married, when there's no one out there to so much as exchange promising glances with. Of course, I know the answer, they're getting married without really knowing who they're marrying. I did that once, and here I am, divorced and back at my father's house, with the only big change in my life being that I gave my old bedroom a makeover. I may be lying here in my room like I did when I was a teenager, but at least I'm lying on my upholstered princess bed with mirrored side tables facing my antique writing desk, staring at the fabulous oil painting I picked up with Haroon at the Indus Valley thesis show last year.

I know it's not Aunty-acceptable, but my marriage ended because we just didn't *like* each other anymore. I'd married London's preeminent party boy. We'd met at a Members Only club where he'd seemed to know everyone and draw people he didn't know to him with his molten hot charm. It was the age at which my friends had been getting married, and when he proposed, it felt like an accomplishment. I didn't know him all that well but he was handsome and popular and always up for a laugh, and I had friends with relationships built on much less. Sadly, it didn't take long to realise he was more substance abuse than substance, that too on the monthly bank transfer his father sent him from home. We parted ways on a sour note. Luckily for me, he had also slept with his yoga instructor (oh, the lack of imagination!) so I left as the clearly wronged party with all the sympathy. Frankly, I didn't really care who he slept with any longer, as long as it wasn't me. I'd never been properly in love with him. I'd been infatuated, as I had been with one or two other guys in my teens and early 20s, but I'd never really been in love.

I thought being married once would kind of take the pressure off but it turns out dating after divorce is hard. At thirty-two, you're neither young nor old, you're caught between crazy coked-up night outs and quiet nights in with friends. Of course, it would help if my friends weren't all married and in the thick of reproducing.

I know everyone feels like this, but my dates have been total weirdos. There'd been the also-divorced British Born Confused Desi ex from college who had relocated to Dubai. After a torrid e-romance, his *gori* girlfriend messaged me to say 'sorry, but we're in love and just waiting for his parents to approve the marriage'. And then there had been the 40-year-old Single Man, who'd seemed wonderful – bright and sophisticated. Just when I was wondering why he hadn't been snapped up yet, I made some completely innocuous comment about how he may want to rethink wearing vintage band t-shirts since it only really suited Zayn Malik, and he went so nuclear, I thought he was going to explode. Last I heard, they're exploring his potential as a WMD.

My phone pings and it hurts my sore muscles to pick it up, though it's actually lying on my chest. It's an iMessage from Saba, the only married friend who still pays me any attention. I'm already so tense about her trying to fix me up with someone tonight. She was pretty wild back in the day but I gently nudged her towards her Sindhi feudal *vadera* hubby. She swore up and down that he wasn't her type but they've been bonking each other senseless ever since. She's just had a baby so I hope it's not a picture of his poo. AGAIN.

**SABA 8:01 PM**

*What you wearing tonight??! Please wear heels and not your weird bargain Uzma Market sandals. I know you have some Gina strappy heels from our Bicester Village trip. See you at 9:30 at the latest! DON'T DITCH!*

**EMAAN**

*IDK! It's just a dinner, right? White shirt and distressed jeans? Uff, please. You say 9:30 and are still standing in your closet wearing just your Spanx at 11 PM.*

**SABA**
*HA HA HA! Bitch. I swear I'll be on time, you know how anal those two are and I really need to get out. ANYWAYS are you excited to meet Mr. Right?*

EMAAN<br>No

**SABA**
*Come ON! He's supposed to be fabulous! Well dressed, educated, right background…*

EMAAN<br>He sounds like a total loser.

**SABA**
*SHUT UP! GO get ready! See you in an HOUR!*

I've met Saba's ideas of 'Mr Right' for me before, and let's just say, they're not worth one's good lingerie. Nonetheless, I fish out a silky top with a low neckline in, what I hope, is an alluring shade of oyster. I'm going to kill Saba if he's as bad as the last one.

Four hours later and I'm waiting to kill Saba. I haven't even met the guy yet because she's yet to show up and introduce us. I arrived as promised at 9:30 and now it's 11 and there's no sign of her. Meanwhile, I'm trapped in a conversation about CPEC and how the influx of Chinese immigrants will affect housing prices. I can process the information, not for nothing did I ace my degree in spite of going out drinking every night, but it's not necessarily what you want to talk about when you've spent an hour blow-drying your hair and contouring your cheeks. If Saba hadn't pressured me into wearing a tight pencil skirt and incredibly uncomfortable if beautiful strappy champagne heels, I'd have been able to slip away far quicker. I'm sipping at my Merlot as fast as possible so I can excuse myself to get a refill, even though it goes straight to my head. The drinks table is a gorgeous slab of raw wood that's been treated to maintain its original beauty. The hosts have exquisite taste – dinner is laid out in the most gorgeous tableware that has been carefully bubble-wrapped and transported, a few dishes at a time, in suitcases from trips abroad. Scented tea lights twinkle around strategically placed vases of lilies and white roses. The chandelier above the table features exposed light bulbs and hanging wires. For a moment I feel like I'm not in Karachi at all and then the post-hair transplant, self-important man who's been droning on about the GDP turns to me and says, 'what do you think?', and I remember that I am very much here. Just as I'm about to slip into a coma from boredom, I smell the possibility of salvation. I hear a deep voice calling someone a *chutiya* and I know Haroon has arrived.

Haroon genuinely falls into the #friendslikefamily hashtag that every social climber is using these days to tag rich people they met two days earlier. Our parents are old Karachi University friends and we've been taking beach trips and club lunches together since I was in my mother's belly. Haroon has a few years on me and is considered good-looking by the marriage mart with his tousled salt and pepper hair, defined cheekbones, Scandinavian height, and the gift for finance with which he converted his family millions into gazillions. For me, his best feature is his sharp and slightly perverse sense of humour. Women from 18 to 48 all squeeze into their tightest midriff-baring blouses for a function if there's a hint of him attending. Yes, yes, people always ask me why I haven't tried my luck with him—the answer to which is that I know him far too well and I can think of smarter ways of spending my time than having my heart dashed on the cliffs on my bestie's compulsive womanising, that is, if I was attracted to him, which I'm not. Haroon isn't even a regular womaniser, by the way. He's so commitment-phobic that he prefers cavorting with married women. I love Haroon but the man needs a therapist more than a girlfriend. For all his toxicity in relationships though, he's the steadiest friend a girl could ask for. He's my happy place.

I'm delighted he's been invited tonight since his last affair caused the end of a rather popular marriage, the soon-to-be ex-wife apparently turning up at his door with a full set of LV luggage and being politely turned away.

I feel him crouch behind me and whisper theatrically, 'You filthy little girl. Are you trying to find a sugar daddy now? I'd tell Uncle, but he'd probably be pleased with the business connections.'

I suppress a giggle and whisper back, 'How many whiskey *paanis* have you had? Your breath could kill a dog.'

Haroon grins and pulls me to a seat in a corner without so much as an 'excuse me'. Taking out a pack of Marlboros, he offers me one.

'It's very uncool to smoke you know, it's all about vaping now,' I pronounce loftily, taking a cigarette.

He's wearing a tailored white shirt, tucked into slightly frayed khakis with his beloved retro Adidas Kicks, sleeves rolled up. He lights both of our cigs, takes a deep puff and exhales.

'Do you even know what vaping is? Now stop being a brat and tell me why you're at this geriatric party and not downing cocktails and conquering hearts somewhere way cooler?'

Grabbing the nearest glass, he flicks ash into someone's black market wine.

I glance around the room, taking in the guests and reply, 'Hardly geriatric, well maybe pushing fifty. Why are you here? Have you finally run out of women in your own age group? Anyways, I'm supposed to meet some guy from London tonight so either I'll be conquering a heart or downing my sorrows in cocktails.'

Even though we've discussed my doomed love life before and Haroon was a principal dancer at my *mehndi*, he's never been completely comfortable about me meeting men. I've always chalked it up to his Big Brother role and being wary of yet another new guy breaking my heart. Frowning into his cigarette, Haroon grimaces and snarks at me, 'expecting to get lucky tonight? That'll be a first'. I'm composing a stinging rebuttal, when I hear a flurry of 'sorry, sorry, I'm so sorry' and turn around.

Saba has finally made her entrance in a Sana Safinaz cocktail dress, bearing a Bottega knot clutch and enveloped in a cloud of Miss Dior. She's apologising loudly between air-kisses, 'Uff, I'm SO late! My night nurse had some last-minute crisis and I got stuck waiting for my MIL to come babysit!' She surveys the room and spots us sitting alone on the table, 'Emaan! You're here! Eww, why are you smoking? And why are you sitting alone with Haroon?' she says, making crazy eyeballs at me.

'We're sitting together because I'm trying to persuade Emaan to finally allow me to make love to her, in mind-blowingly filthy ways,' he says, with a straight face, to which Saba, who's met him often, rolls her eyes. 'Wait, why are you so late? Where's that degenerate husband of yours?'

He heads off to speak to him. Saba starts smoothing the crinkles out of my top like a monkey grooming its young. I bat her hands way before she starts checking for lice. 'Saba, for God's sake,' I say, 'I'm not your baby!'

'You certainly eat like him!' she says, rubbing at what seems to be a food stain. 'So, did you meet

Mustafa?' she said, her voice dropping. 'Isn't he just so yummy? I love that accent and I heard he's bought a lovely house in Clifton! Not bad, eh?'

Saba's eyes dart around the room sizing up the situation.

Suddenly feeling tired and wanting my bed, I crankily tell her, 'What guy? Honestly Saba, what a waste of time! I can't believe how late you are. There's no one here under forty and I've been listening to people discuss the Panama Papers all night. I really hate you.'

Unperturbed, she grabs the remains of my smoke and takes a deep drag.

'There! He's right there!' she says, pointing and waving enthusiastically at someone in a smoky corner. 'He's divine. Go marry him immediately so I have an excuse to buy some killer outfits!'

I can see the man in question coming towards us now and I squint, trying to get better visuals through the mood lighting and puffs of smoke.

I find myself studying an immaculately groomed individual of average brown man height, wearing a dark single-breasted suit with a dark shirt, topped with a perfectly gelled coiffure. The decreasing distance shows a face that has smaller pores than mine and the accompanying features are soft and amiable. Not bad, but giving off a metrosexual vibe which I don't know how I feel about.

Seeing Saba, he saunters over, and out comes the Black Amex of accents – British boarding school.

'Saba, darling, you made it! You look yummy.'

'I'm Mustafa,' he says, turning to me, 'but everyone calls me Musti. So, you're the famous Emaan? I've been promised some witty banter! This one talks about you a great deal.' I blush, thinking about Saba's attempts at palming me off on this man, on any man really.

I smile awkwardly and reply, 'Oh! Well I hope the real thing doesn't disappoint!', tugging at my shirt now and feeling like a bug under a microscope.

Musti laughs. I see his eyes roaming over me appraisingly and catching the food stain on my top that Saba was picking at earlier. Reaching over, he stabs at it with a finger and says, 'Had a misunderstanding with the fricassee? I had some personal issues as well but looks like you took a beating.'

I realise Saba has nicely sauntered off, leaving us to awkwardly flirt alone in a semi-private corner of the room. 'Everyone knows that chickens play dirty. You should see me at the local sushi joint. I'm deadly with chopsticks.'

I'm rewarded with a laugh. While he isn't my type, the needy side of me hums with pleasure at his appreciation. He slides close enough for me to smell his aftershave and admire his gleaming white teeth. I press my lips together to make sure my food and cig breath doesn't hit him.

'Then we should go to dinner to see these chopstick martial art skills.'

He rests his hand lightly on my lower back now, something I hate since it makes me self-conscious about my love handles. I hold my breath. I'm enjoying his attention and the light banter typically missing in Karachi hook-ups, which tend to start with small talk and end with a hastily booked Sindh Club room after sufficient alcohol has been consumed. Musti may be coming on too strong. but it's been so long since I've felt desired by someone who isn't a freak show, I'm willing to be less cautious than usual.

I look around the room and see Haroon speaking to and quite possibly chatting up some pretty young thing and Saba standing with her husband, giggling. Sick of being a third wheel, I galvanise myself with a large slug of vodka tonic.

'Are we talking date night or a friendly dinner? Because I need to know if I'm performing ninja moves post sushi.'

If that doesn't get his attention, nothing will. Sure enough, he blinks and a slow smile spreads. He comes close enough to whisper in my ear.

'Sounds dangerous, let's make it dinner and drinks at my place then. Actually, if you're free right now, shall we go for a nightcap?'

Here is the dating decision every single girl over a certain age has to make. You can't keep up the virginal ingénue pretence post thirty (particularly post-divorce), but there's a fine line between sophisticated and slutty. I've been good for long enough to cross it tonight. I lean in further, allowing enough body contact to make my agreement clear and whisper my response.

'No, I'm done drinking for the night, but I can be tempted with something sweet. Sadly, the cake didn't do it for me.'

Musti smiles against my neck, and then full-on kisses me. More forward than romantic, I am taken aback by this sudden PDA. Musti pulls away. I think I can hear titters, though maybe that's just my paranoia. The last time I had no-strings-attached-sex was the previous December season, when a nice American wedding guest allowed me an anonymous physical release. With someone local, wondering if the town will find out about your one-night stand can really kill your orgasm. I take a deep breath and throw my *izzat* to the wind. He takes my hand to lead me out.

Before we even reach the front door we hear a discreet cough and I feel someone grab my shoulder. Haroon's voice booms out.

'Musti! Fantastic to see you again, I see you've met my sister from another mister, Emaan.'

This stops Musti and me in our hormonal tracks.

'Err, yes. How are you, mate? Didn't know you two were friendly,' Musti says, letting go of my hand.

He steps back discreetly, allowing Haroon the alpha male position. I scowl at him and try to gain some control of the hook-up I can feel crumbling around me. I catch Haroon's eye.

'Heyyy, we were just leaving! Let's catch up tomorrow?' I link my arm through Musti's again and try to pull him towards the door.

Nope. My silent protest has zero effect. 'I told your dad I'd drop you home tonight. I'm sure Musti understands. Come on, let's go now.'

Musti frowns but doesn't push it, he gently pulls his arm away and bids us adieu, 'Yes, I'm sure. Emaan, it was lovely to meet you, I'll ping you about dinner. We can pick up where we left off.'

He gives me a chaste peck on the cheek and a subtle squeeze of the hand. With a wink, he walks back into the room, presumably to find a woman who doesn't come with her own personal bodyguard.

Haroon grabs me and roughly pulls me out of the house. My mood has gone from lightly buzzed to full-on sulky. He stops when we get to the main entrance, a circular driveway in front, dotted with various Land Cruisers and Mercs.

'What the hell! That was really embarrassing, Haroon! I can make my own decisions and you are hardly one to pull some Moral Police shit on me. You're always sabotaging me! There hasn't been a single romantic possibility that you haven't shot down since my ex-husband. What is your problem?'

I realise I sound rather more petulant than righteous, but really, of all the things Haroon is, a puritanical hypocrite has never before been one of them. For a society filled with secret swinger clubs and multiple dating apps, it's still unseemly for a woman to publicly swipe right.

'Shut up, Emaan. I can't believe how stupid you are sometimes. That guy is such a dick! He thinks he's

God's gift to women, he talks about them like they're shit and he would have blabbed to the entire town about your hook-up! I felt sick watching you kiss that bastard. I'm just looking out for you! Like I always have. I do want you to be happy but you definitely wouldn't be as another notch on his bedpost.'

I feel a slow blush come over me. What he's saying sounds totally plausible. But I can't say anything to him now that he's in the middle of shouting me down to size. We've had our disagreements, but they've never resulted in him raising his voice. The drivers and armed guards are openly gawking and enjoying some entertainment while waiting for their charges to finally leave.

'Haroon', I say, 'you're my friend, not my keeper.' I speak slowly, trying to keep my voice steady, embarrassed to find that I can feel a lump forming in my throat, which I frantically clear, 'I don't see how my happiness lies in sitting around like Ms Havisham while you're bonking everyone like Christian Grey! Just because *you* want to be alone for the rest of your life doesn't mean that *I* want the same.'

Haroon looks aghast. 'Is that what you think of me?'

I shrug non-committedly. I am expecting him to be angry but this is something else, he looks... disappointed. I turn away before he can see that I'm on the verge of tears. 'I'm going back in', I say.

'OK, Emaan,' he says, 'you do what you want.'

He heads to his car. I return to the party, by now a sad, extinguished affair, which is how I feel about most parties without Haroon being around to liven them up. Musti comes up to me, looking for Haroon over my shoulder and smiling hopefully. I ignore him. On second viewing, he looks like the sleaze Haroon said he was. I ask Saba if her driver will drop me home, she's about to insist as usual that I stay, but she sees the look on my face and knows that I mean business. I sit in the backseat of their plush car driving through a still-bustling, late-night Karachi, crying as quietly as I can.

Two days later, I'm still in my PJs though it's almost dinnertime. I've spent most of the weekend lying in bed staring vacantly at my laptop scrolling through mindless clickbait. On Instagram, I spotted a picture of Musti canoodling with a twenty-something at some seedy party the night after we met. I shudder at the enormity of the mistake I could have made. I've had no word yet from Haroon in spite of sending him a string of friendly emojis.

My phone pings, it's my father, 'Emaan! Yusuf Uncle, Bubbly Aunty, and Haroon called to say they're on their way.'

Haroon? My heart does a strange flip hearing his name. I spring out of bed and leap into a quick shower, frantically applying some tinted moisturiser, cream blush, and a swipe of mascara. Haroon has seen me in my pyjamas before, he's seen me with bits of crud around my eyes. He has seen me in all stages of slothfulness—I don't know why I'm spritzing the perfume I had specially made for me on my pleasure points.

I'm actually having to give myself a pep talk to calm down—it's only Haroon and his parents, who I've only met a million times already, when I open my bedroom door and stumble backwards because he's standing right outside.

'Umm, hello! I'm not that late. They didn't need to send you to get me,' I say.

Haroon runs a hand through his hair, taking a step forward and resting his arms on the doorframe, effectively blocking my way. He's in a well-worn t-shirt and track pants with Bata flipflops, smelling of the Body Shop shower gel he sends me into the shop to buy for him because it's bright pink. With his arms stretched, I can see his muscles and toned stomach. He still hasn't said anything and is just staring at me.

'Emaan, I need to speak to you. Before you come down.'

He pushes his way into my room and walks around, absentmindedly picking up my assorted knick-knacks to occupy his hands. I hesitate and then close the door behind me.

I clear my throat and break the silence by saying, 'You know, you're the only boy who's allowed in my room. Papa would go ballistic if anyone else ever came up here. Just you.'

He puts my books down and turns to look at me, his tall frame looming. I stop rambling. I realise I'm holding my breath, so nervous am I about whatever he has to say to me in private.

'I'm getting married,' he says. 'My parents are going to tell Uncle over dinner, but I thought... well I wanted to tell you first.'

'Oh!' I respond, 'Well, congrats! It's about time, I guess.'

I answer automatically but my stomach drops hearing the news. I feel a weight pushing down on my chest. I draw a ragged breath and bite my lip.

Haroon looks at me, clocks my reaction, and crosses the room, taking my hands. I pull back a little but he tightens his grip and pulls me to him, tucking me into his chest and fitting me in as if I was made to fill his empty spaces. I relax and mould myself inside, my face filled with his scent and skin, my arms around his chest and back. He puts his hand behind my head, the other pushing inside my shirt and touching the bare skin of my back.

We stay like this for seconds till he tugs my hair and makes me look up.

'I'm sorry, I should have said something sooner, done something sooner.' He whispers against my lips.

I feel frozen and confused.

Suddenly, we hear my father coming up the stairs, his distinctive plodding outside my door but we don't break contact.

Knocking, he asks 'Is everything OK? Emaan? Come down, everyone is waiting! I'm going to go look for Haroon, he said he was going to get you.'

Haroon takes my face in his hand and smiles. 'I wish I wasn't shit with women,' he says, opening the door. He starts to walk down the stairs, leaving me breathless.

Damn.

When did I fall in love with him?

###

London streets whizz by the window of my taxi; roads sleek with rain, a spring chill still in the air, signs for Easter sales in shop fronts. It's cold and not the ideal time to be here, but I couldn't stay in Karachi where the Who's Who were preparing to attend Haroon's wedding.

I don't know much about her, I didn't ask anyone anything, I didn't forensically examine social media accounts. I just know that she's not me. I couldn't escape the wedding news. Every Aunty was bursting with details, from the choice of event planners and the caterer's menus, the invitations printed in India, the singers and bands being flown in, to the bootleggers bribed to ensure only the best sparkling wine for Haroon's wife. It seems you can arrange the wedding of the year in barely a few months when you have the financial and social backing.

Friends and family were stunned when I announced that I wouldn't be able to make it to my oldest friend's wedding, even if it was for a once-in-a-lifetime job interview. Haroon didn't say anything, I didn't expect him to. We'd not been in touch since all of this happened, there seemed to be nothing to say any longer.

After *that* conversation with Haroon, I'd dragged myself downstairs and smiled robotically when the wedding news was announced. His parents were ecstatic, he was finally settling down. I couldn't look at him but felt his eyes like pinpricks on my body.

He left town the next day, 'travelling for work,' he said. And that marked the beginning of us avoiding each other. We were both very good at it. I tried to pin down when I'd started feeling more for him than friendship, maybe after my divorce when I'd be feeling desperately lonely and self-piteous at 3 a.m. and he'd pick me up for ice cream and coffee. Or perhaps the first time I had to go to a party alone, nervous without a plus-one, worried about what people were saying about me and he'd spent the whole night by my side, spilling secrets into my ear to distract me. Or the times I'd call him to come over at midnight to watch a movie, both of us in our PJs, eating kettle corn with sticky fingers.

He became my person, and though he usually had some sort of relationship on the go, it never spilled over into our special space. Till he announced his marriage.

I'd turned on my laptop that very night and updated my CV, emailing it to everyone I knew outside Pakistan. Within a few days, an old college friend working at Facebook had messaged me saying there was an opening at Instagram's London office in Communications and that they wanted to talk to me. By some miracle, my finance and writing background, and love for social media mixed with some sort of diversity push at Instagram meant they liked me. Today had been the last interview and it didn't go so badly. It was ridiculous that instead of thinking of a career – finally – that might actually mean something to me, I was moping over a boy.

My phone pings, I fish it out of my bag quickly, thinking it might be something about my interview and when I see the message I stare, feeling my heart beat out of chest.

**Haroon**
*Hi*

**Emaan**
*Hi*

**Haroon**
*What are you doing?*

**Emaan**
*Nothing, in a taxi, getting back to the flat. Wasn't it the nikkah part of your wedding today?*

**Haroon**
*Yup*

**Emaan**
*Well, congratulations!*

**Haroon**
*Yup*

**Emaan**
*Look, I'm sorry I couldn't be there but it's for the best. I'll talk to you soon but I'm home now and have to pay the taxi. Good luck with the wedding, OK?*

I turn my phone off before I can see his reply and put it in my bag. I'm thanking the driver and opening the taxi door to the narrow street our flat is located on, when I hear a familiar voice.

'Here, let me. It's bloody raining, so hurry up and come out. I'm freezing.'

Haroon grins nervously at me. My brain fills with white static and my smile splits my face open, the silliness of it echoing on his face now. He more or less pulls me out of the car.

'What! What are you doing here? You're supposed to be getting married!' I stutter at him as he pulls me into him.

It's so cold I can't feel my fingers but I can feel the warmth of this embrace.

'I didn't. I got on a plane instead. I don't even have bags! We're going to have to go buy me some underwear. Now, kiss me, you stupid girl. I love you. I've loved you for so long.'

And so, I did.

# The Mughal Empire

## Saniyya Gauhar

*"Miss Bingley was very deeply mortified by Darcy's marriage"*

—Pride and Prejudice

It was a truth universally acknowledged and widely gossiped about through the length and breadth of high society, that Kamila Mughal, the proud, beautiful publisher of the glossy society magazine, *Pink*, had been deeply humiliated.

Only two weeks ago, Faisal Dayyan, one of Pakistan's most eligible bachelors and the man who had been the object of her unwavering attention and very obvious admiration for the better part of a decade, had married Erum Bilal, a girl from Islamabad whom no one had ever heard of before.

This was a source of even greater horror to her than the fact that Kamila's own brother and Faisal's best friend, Chengiz, had married Erum's elder sister Jahanara, meaning herself and the unknowns were now related, no less.

Both couples were currently honeymooning in the Seychelles while Kamila was seated in her office overseeing the layout of the magazine feature on the double wedding!

Upon entering her all-glass office wearing her darkest Chanel sunglasses, she was confronted with inflated images of the wretched wedding, as her graphic designer had helpfully enlarged his proposed layout of the feature on a large screen. The remaining photographs were left on her desk for approval and it had taken every ounce of courage to bring herself to look at them.

Jealousy is a lonely emotion that cannot and must not be shared with anyone. Kamila hadn't expressed her bitter disappointment. True, she may have said a word or two about the unsuitability of Jahanara and Erum but everyone felt that way about them. Her own sense of being overlooked by Faisal was too shameful to put into words. It was too private, too primal, too ugly to even discuss with her closest friends. It must be treated like a terrible secret.

And so, upon entering her office, Kamila pulled down every single blind.

A photograph of Erum in her breathtaking wedding couture caught Kamila's attention first.

*That outfit alone would have cost at least twenty lakhs.*

She thought about how, before marrying up, Erum and her sisters would get their clothes embroidered by cheap *karigar*s in Islamabad's F-10 market who copied designer outfits from magazines.

*From rags to riches.*

And what riches! For not only had Faisal's mother assembled a *barri* comprising outfits from some of Pakistan's top designers, she had also flown Erum and her mother, Zehra Bilal, to London in the Dayyans' private Gulfstream. Here, she had bought Erum luxuries that most girls could only dream of: handbags from Hermès, Chanel, Bottega Veneta and Prada; shoes for every possible occasion in an assortment of styles and colours from Manolo Blahnik, Christian Louboutin, Jimmy Choo, Saint Laurent, Roger Vivier and Dior; lingerie from Rigby & Peller, Agent Provocateur and La Perla, and a designer wardrobe from some of the finest stores on Sloane Street. To add to this was a diamond set from Graff that Erum had worn at her wedding. And how it had glittered!

It was this last thought that broke Kamila's inward composure. She felt her stomach lurch at the reminder of the glint of the pavé diamond necklace.

*It should have been me*.

The thought was not unreasonable in her circles. Erum's father was some sort of undistinguished civil servant, whereas Kamila was the daughter of millionaire businessman, Jahangir Mughal.

She had known Faisal since they were children. As her brother's best friend, he'd always been around. Unbeknownst to him, she had decided fairly early on that she would marry him and only him. He was handsome and charming, and also sole heir to one of the largest fortunes in Pakistan. The Dayyans owned practically everything and were cultured and enlightened to boot. In short, Faisal was perfect husband material. How proud she would have been to walk into a room as his wife—everyone would have looked at them in admiration and envy!

How had her plans gone so horribly wrong?

*'Islamabad,'* she thought to herself. *'The trouble started when we moved to this awful city.'*

A year ago, Kamila's father had accepted the position of Special Advisor to the Prime Minister on Finance. This had caused dismay among his wife and daughters as it involved moving to the capital, which they considered a small, stiflingly dull city populated by tedious provincials. The situation was made slightly more palatable by the fact that Jahangir Mughal had bought the largest, grandest house on the Margalla Road, one that, in his daughters' view, befitted their status. The Mughals became the fulcrum of Islamabad high society—such as it was—more or less the moment they moved in, with invitations to their house the most sought after in the city.

Amongst their first visitors were Fahad and Zehra Bilal, who had wasted no time in introducing them to their five daughters: Jahanara, Erum, Maya, Kiran and Lamia. That was when Chengiz met Jahanara and became positively smitten, much to the horror of his mother and both his sisters, Kamila and Laila. Our own flesh and blood, they lamented, being taken in by this gold-digger! However, their attempts at talking sense into him had failed. Chengiz was a reserved young man, innocent of any understanding of social hierarchy. He had never shown any serious interest in anyone until he laid eyes on Jahanara, whom he saw as a breath of fresh air. His mother's tears and the long chats with his sisters amounted to nothing and so they were forced to swallow their pride in a grand gulp and accept the match with as much good grace as could be mustered.

Soon after they had moved into the big house on Margalla Road, Faisal had flown in on some business and had stayed with them as the Serena was fully booked by the entourage of a visiting head of state. It was during the course of this visit that Chengiz introduced him to Erum, Jahanara's younger sister. The rest, as they say, is history.

*Those Bilal girls worked fast.*

Kamila's thoughts were disturbed by the clickety-clack of approaching stilettoes in the corridor outside. Flinging open the door, her elder sister Laila entered in her customary cloud of Chanel N°5.

Laila wore an immaculate white lawn *kurta* with matching cigarette pants, a red Hermès Birkin cradled on her arm. Her hair was immaculately blow-dried and her earlobes flashed the fire of the two-carat diamond solitaire studs that Jahangir Mughal had given his daughters to mark the occasion of their brother's wedding. Accompanying her was one of Kamila's closest friends, Murad Aziz.

'Ouch!' Laila exclaimed, seeing the enlarged photographs on the SmartBoard. 'That's a bit in-your-face, isn't it?'

'Ouch is the word!' said Murad dramatically. 'Sweetie, do you really think that plastering life-sized images of Faisal and his provincial bride all over your wall is going to help you move on?'

Murad was a successful fashion designer and man about town. He and Kamila had been BFFs since school. Though he recognised that she could be standoffish, catty and snobbish, he found these traits amusing and wouldn't have it any other way.

'This is for *Pink*. There's nothing for me to move on from,' Kamila replied petulantly.

'Oh, come on, sweetie.'

Kamila winced. The three-day events for the double wedding had been the hardest of her life. Not only had she endured the pain of seeing Faisal with Erum, she had been even more mortified at the thought of being perceived as a woman scorned. The very idea was repugnant. She had, therefore, made up her mind to sparkle and pretend that she was having a marvellous time in an effort to dispel the notion that she had ever held a candle for the groom.

'Ooh!' squealed Laila at the photographs on Kamila's desk. 'Make sure you print nice ones of me!'

'There are ten more albums on over there if you want to see,' Kamila said dryly, indicating her coffee table. 'Cut the nonsense!' Murad said as he and Laila sat down on the two chairs opposite Kamila's desk. '*Everyone* knows that you wanted to marry him!'

Murad's brazenness rendered Kamila temporarily speechless.

'I don't think *everyone*...' she eventually said.

'*Everyone* knew,' Murad said sharply. 'Everyone who's anyone, that is. But your magnificent performance at Faisal's wedding went a long way in confusing people.'

Murad immediately jumped up and grabbed an album each.

'Oh my gosh, Anaya looks so fat in this one—you must print it!' squealed Laila delighted.

'Eww, what's Sakina Aunty wearing?' Murad said, jubilantly. 'Print this too!'

Ordinarily, Kamila would have gleefully gone over every detail of the society photos with a merciless eye, delivering cutting asides all the while but today her heart just wasn't in it.

A loud *ping* made everyone jump. Laila fished her phone out of her bag.

'Ooh! I got a WhatsApp message from Chengiz!' she said.

'*Seychelles is beautiful. Jahanara sends her love xx*'

'He sent a picture! Look...' She handed the phone to Kamila who felt an immense wave of irritation when she saw the photograph of her brother and the woman who was now her sister-in-law smiling on the beach.

'She's wearing Valentino sandals!' said Laila. 'Remember those hideous chappals she was wearing from Paradise Shoe Palace when we first met her?'

'Just imagine!' Kamila sneered.

'These convent girls are really *tez*,' Laila said, not for the first time, as she put her phone away.

'They know how to hook guys. They can flirt with a man with simply *a look*. We're really straightforward in comparison!'

'I heard that Humayun Uncle is transferring their 16th Arrondissement apartment in Paris in Erum's name. As a wedding present,' said Murad.

Kamila's heart sank further. *It should have been me*.

'OK listen, we need to stop talking about how wonderful the Dayyans are,' said Murad decidedly. 'Kamila sweetie, I've been in this godforsaken city for two weeks now at your request…'

'You're not leaving!' Kamila said coolly.

'Eventually, love, I have to return to Karachi—I have a business to run. And, even though you never actually articulated it, you and I both know the reason why you wanted me to stay…'

'What's that? To cheer me up after my heart was left broken?' Kamila said flippantly with a smile.

'Not your heart, sweetie. Your pride.'

'My pride?'

'Yes, my dear, your pride,' said Murad. 'If it had been your heart, trust me you'd have recovered by now. In fact, if you ask me, a wounded ego is much worse than a wounded heart.'

Kamila stared icily at Murad as she tried to think of a fitting response.

'But rest assured, I'm not leaving until both your ego *and* your pride have been restored to their former glory! And since I'm loath to stay in this dreadful city for longer than necessary, we have to go into urgent damage control mode.'

Kamila smiled thinly. 'I'm fine. You said yourself that my behaviour at the wedding was impeccable.'

'Yes, but that was just a performance, like acting,' said Murad. 'Now, we have to wage a two-pronged strategy to rehabilitate you, internally and externally. Let's call it Operation Rehab. Number one: the external element—optics. You need to see and be seen. Sparkle. Socialise. Soon, people will doubt that Faisal was anything more than a family friend in your eyes.'

'Socializing in Islamabad is death by boredom,' said Kamila.

'I concur,' chimed in Laila, 'This place is seriously dull. Excited Aunties. NGO types. Random *gora* diplos. Sleazy MNA Uncles…'

'Well… do your best,' Murad said. 'Number two: the *internal* element. Broaden your horizons. Try and *meet* people. This world is full of interesting people even if they aren't all richer than Croesus.'

'I've met everyone there is to meet.'

'No, darling, I mean *really* meet people. You've been mentally unavailable to everyone because of your obsession with Mr Dayyan. You may find, once you start to look, that there are, in fact, plenty of fish in the sea.'

'That's actually not true, Murad,' Laila said, happy to hold forth on a subject which was a special area of interest for her. 'There are hardly any nice guys around. Look at all the unmarried girls!'

'There are loads of guys,' said Kamila frostily. 'But nobody that *I* can marry.'

'What do you mean?' Murad said. 'You know everyone, you're wealthy in your own right and don't need anything from anyone—you have more choices than you think.'

'No, Murad, it's *harder* for someone like me,' Kamila said in a patronizing tone. 'A woman should never marry beneath her social class. A rich woman can only marry a rich man or the son of a rich man if she wants to be happy, that is. And there are few people around who are as rich or richer than Daddy. And so, for someone like me, the pond is actually a puddle.'

She folded her arms and looked at him fixedly.

'Sweetheart! Those views are really outdated!' said Murad. 'This is 2017. And you have a degree from Princeton! What happened to your dream of being an author? I can't believe you're talking like this!'

'It's true,' Laila added. 'No matter what career a woman has, in this country, you're either known as someone's daughter or someone's wife. That's why I never even bothered working.'

'Ladies, if you put all these restrictions on yourselves, then yes, neither of you ever had a puddle with a single fish in it to begin with!'

'*I'm* married,' objected Laila. '*I* found a fish in the puddle.'

'You compromised,' Kamila said.

'I did not!' Laila exclaimed, outraged.

'You married the first rich guy you met after college and bagged him without thinking. But look at your fish—he wakes up at noon, rolls into the office at two, stays till three and is drunk by four. And you spend most of your time with us.'

'Are you saying I should get a divorce?' Laila countered.

Kamila shrugged her shoulders.

'Urgh! This conversation has become way too serious,' said Laila rolling her eyes. She clattered her way to the small fridge in the corner of the room. 'I'm hungry. Do you have celery? Ooh! Yes, you do!'

She bit into the celery as if it were a bar of chocolate. 'My trainer says I just need to lose five pounds more.'

'Uff, please Laila!' Murad said. 'If you lose any more weight, you'll get the lollipop look!'

'I know you think that just because I'm married I can let myself go—but that's not true,' Laila said. 'Besides, you just said I should get a divorce. So now I need to look my best if I have to hook another guy!'

'Laila, nobody said anything of the sort.' Murad rolled his eyes.

'Not only that,' continued Laila, 'but in case you'd forgotten, Maryam Qasim is getting married in four days and I can't look like a beach ball. What are you going to wear to the wedding?'

Kamila scowled. 'Oh *please*! I'm not going to *that* wedding! I hardly know her.'

'Oh, come on, we meet her all the time' Laila said between mouthfuls of celery. 'And Mama has extended her stay in Italy and won't be back in time for the wedding. She says we have to represent her *and*—don't freak out—that we have to go over to their place either today or tomorrow with a nice present, preferably a carpet.'

'What?' Kamila said in horror. 'Why can't we just send it with the driver?'

'Because Maryam's father is the new Interior Minister so Mama said we have to go to their house and give the present personally. And attend the wedding.'

'See and be seen!' said Murad brightly.

'Murad—you haven't been to a real Isloo wedding—you only see and are seen by judgemental, sanctimonious Aunties!'

'Sweetie, this wedding won't be that dull. Trust me,' Murad said. 'Yours truly has designed the bride's *mehndi* outfit and I'm told loads of people from Karachi and Lahore are coming. And if Zehra Bilal, your new relative, is sending her three remaining unmarried daughters to the bride's house every day so that they can feature prominently in all the *mehndi* dances, believe me, this isn't an event to dismiss so lightly! That woman is the best social barometer of everything!'

'Not only that,' said Laila, 'But Mrs Bilal is also the major-domo of the wedding! She's helping Naheed Aunty with everything!'

The acerbic comment forming on Kamila's lips was interrupted by her phone buzzing.

'It's from *him!*' she said, surprised. Her heart started beating annoyingly fast.

'Ooh, what does he say?' Laila asked walking behind Kamila's chair to read the message. 'Is he fed up of Erum already?'

Kamila read the message aloud:

*'Kamila, please do me a small favour. As you know, I'm a private person and feel uncomfortable having images of my wedding splashed across the society pages. I would, therefore, be grateful if you would not cover the wedding in Pink. I know you'll understand.*

*Best,*
*Faisal'*

'He thinks he's Prince William!' Laila jibed. 'Going on about being private!'

'How should I respond?' Kamila asked, typing out her reply. 'How's this?'

*'Dear Faisal,*
*Of course, I understand. I'll scrap the feature. However, please do me a favour and explain this to your MIL. She's sent me ten photo albums and made me promise to do a cover story. Since she's*

*also my brother's MIL, you understand that the situation is delicate. x'*

'Ooh! Good reply!' Laila said, smiling. 'Press Send.'

'No, Kamila!' Murad said firmly. 'Keep it short. Just write, "Sure." One word. Nothing else.'

'What?'

'Don't give him that much importance by writing reams and reams.'

Kamila hesitated. Reluctantly, she deleted her message and wrote, *'Sure.'*

The curt response left her feeling most unsatisfied. Murad stood up and quickly switched off the projector. 'Uff! Thank goodness! Now, please go to Mariam Qasim's house with the present, attend all her functions, dress to kill and sparkle!'

'But we can't stay too long,' Laila said, playing with her Cartier Love bracelets, 'because then people will think we have nothing else to do.'

###

Maryam Qasim's place epitomised a *shaadi ka ghar.* Guests strolled in and out; electricians were busy putting up fairy lights; a *shamiana* was being erected in the garden; white sheets covered the floor of the lounge where two *mehndiwalis* sat applying intricate designs surrounded by ladies waiting their turn; the dining table was laden with silver chafing dishes of *haleem, biryani, halwa, puri* and small clay bowls of *kheer.* A samovar of Kashmiri *chai* was on one of the tables as well as baskets containing colourful glass bangles, multi-coloured silk *dupattas* and an assortment of *mithai.* The latest Indian film song was blaring as girls and boys practiced the synchronised dances meant to entertain the guests at the *mehndi.* It was open house and everyone was welcome to partake in the jolly chaos.

'I can't believe we're doing this!' whispered Kamila grumpily to Laila as they strutted up the driveway. Their driver followed holding the carpet which was wrapped in a shiny green cloth.

'Did you remember to put Daddy's card on the present?' Laila hissed.

'Yes, yes,' said Kamila, irritated.

'So, do you really think I should get a divorce?' Laila whispered.

Kamila rolled her eyes. 'Not *now,* Laila!' she said in an angry whisper.

Maryam Qasim saw the girls from her lounge window and excitedly told her mother. Naheed Qasim rushed to the front door to greet them.

'Hello girls! How wonderful to see you!'

The girls smiled their standard fake smiles. They took in the buzzing activity around them with mild disdain and the driver was relieved of the carpet by one of the bearers.

'It's such a shame your mother can't come,' Naheed said sadly. 'But I told her, you have to send the girls!'

Kamila and Laila managed a smile but didn't reply. Of course, the Qasims wanted a Mughal to attend their wedding, thought Kamila. It was a matter of social prestige!

'Girls, please come and put on some *mehndi*?'

They politely declined. Naheed Qasim then entreated them to try the *haleem* assuring them it was to die for, which they also declined. She then picked up two sets of glass bangles from a basket and gave them to Kamila and Laila who received them with muted contempt.

She then ushered them into the lounge where they were somewhat taken aback by the rather effusive greeting from the bride-to-be who hugged them both and thanked them profusely for coming. Seconds later, they were gushingly greeted by Kiran and Lamia, their new sisters-in-law.

'Kamila! Laila!' they squealed in unison. Laila and Kamila winced as they were treated to kisses and hugs.

'Ooh! Kiran look!' cried Lamia. 'Zaki and Adnan are here! Come! Let's go bug them!'

The two of them scurried towards two young men who had just arrived, leaving Kamila and Laila with the bride-to-be.

'Please take a seat,' said Mariam gesturing towards one of the sofas. 'I think you might know some people…'

No sooner had she said this, a deep-pitched female voice interrupted, 'Oh my gosh, Kamila?'

Kamila looked up and saw Malia Ahmad, whom she often met on the Lahore social circuit, walking into the lounge barefoot, wearing a crushed lawn outfit with her hair in a messy topknot. Her husband Ayyan was heir to a textile empire.

'Malia! What are you doing here?' asked Kamila, surprised to see 'one of her own.'

'Maryam's my cousin, *yaar,*' replied Malia. 'Ayyan and I drove down yesterday but he wants to go back to Lahore and return day after tomorrow for the *mehndi*! Uff, it's impossible to tear a Lahori away from Lahore—even though it's a furnace these days!'

'Lahore is Lahore!' Ayyan said from one of the sofas where he was relaxing. 'There's nothing to do here!'

'Shut up, Ayyan!' Malia said, 'Look at the hills!'

Malia then took Kamila and Laila aside and said sotto voce: '*Achha yaar*, we didn't get a chance to talk after Faisal's wedding, but are you okay? I mean, we all thought the two of you would marry?'

Kamila blushed. 'I don't know why everybody keeps saying that!' she whispered back. 'He was just a friend! If I had wanted to marry him, I would have.'

Malia nodded. 'Yes, of course. Well, I mean, people talk nonsense. Don't worry about it,' she said kindly. 'I'm going to go try the *haleem*. Ayyan, come, get up! Let's have some *haleem*.'

'I don't want *haleem,* I want a Kobe steak,' complained Ayyan as he followed Malia into the dining room next door.

'Shut up, Ayyan! This is a *shaadi ka ghar!* Where are you going to find a Kobe steak?'

At that moment, they were assailed by the sound of a shrill voice: 'Girls!'

It was Zehra Bilal. She hurriedly walked towards them and nearly tripped on her oversized *dupatta* in the process.

'Do we make a run for it?' Kamila asked Laila snidely.

'Too late,' said Laila between gritted teeth.

Too late indeed, for they were soon being greeted by perfumed hugs and kisses.

'How wonderful to see you! I haven't seen you both since the wedding! Kamila *beta,* did you get the wedding albums I sent you?'

'Yes, Aunty' replied Kamila, her voice like steel. 'But Faisal messaged and said he doesn't want any photos published.'

'Really? Why?' Mrs. Bilal was incredulous.

'He says he wants privacy.'

'Privacy? What nonsense! A wedding's such a public thing!'

'Maybe he's embarrassed?' suggested Kamila coolly. 'I can't think why.'

Mrs. Bilal sighed. 'Anyway, Kamila, it's your turn next,' she said putting her arm around Kamila.

Kamila felt a pang of disgust. 'For what?' she replied, even though she knew perfectly well what Mrs Bilal meant.

'Why marriage, of course! You're almost thirty, *beta*,' said Mrs Bilal earnestly. 'I told your mother that Kamila is now no different from one of my own daughters and I won't rest till she finds herself a good husband!'

Kamila was aghast; she couldn't decide whether she was more appalled by Mrs Bilal's familiarity or the suggestion that she was now like one of her daughters!

Mrs Bilal went on. 'I'm so glad you girls came today. Kamila, you *must* take part in the dances!'

'I don't dance,' Kamila said, visibly annoyed.

'Oh, come on! Be a sport! Maryam *beta,*' she said. 'Please make sure that Kamila's included in one of the dances!'

She rushed off, leaving Kamila absolutely dumbfounded. Maryam, delighted at the prospect of Kamila dancing at her *mehndi*, grabbed her hand and started pulling her towards the corner of the lounge where the dance practice was taking place. 'Oh, come on, Kamila! It'll be fun!'

Kamila was flabbergasted. She was not used to people being so overly familiar with her.

'No, Maryam! I don't dance. I just came to drop off the present.'

'Oh, shut up, Kamila!' Malia said as she walked back into the lounge carrying a bowl of *haleem.* 'We need a partner for Siraj.'

'Who is Siraj?' Kamila asked, exasperated.

'He's my cousin. I think he was also in school with you. That's what he said.'

'I don't remember a Siraj.'

'That's probably because you never noticed,' said a man's voice from behind her.

She turned and found herself face to face with a man who was tall, handsome in a rugged sort of way, and oddly familiar.

'Er…Siraj Khan?' she ventured.

'Kamila Mughal,' he smiled.

'Um…it's been years,' said Kamila with a forced smile.

The last time she had even noticed Siraj Khan, he had been a foot shorter than her and had accidentally spilt potassium permanganate on her uniform when they were in the tenth grade. This had caused such consternation in both that neither had spoken to the other for the remainder of their time at school, Kamila out of contempt and Siraj out of embarrassment.

'Rest assured, I'm not holding any purple liquids in my hands today,' he said, holding his hands up.

Kamila's fake society-smile grew wider. 'Yes. Well, thank heaven for that.'

He laughed.

Malia explained the dance. 'It's a couples' dance and there'll be eight of us, four guys and four girls. Me, you, Kiran, and Lamia. The guys are Ayyan, Zaki, Adnan, and Siraj. It's very easy. Don't worry, none of us are great dancers. Just follow my lead.'

Kamila could not believe this was happening and was even more irritated at her complete inability to excuse herself.

'I just need to make a phone call. I'll be back,' Kamila said.

'You have two minutes,' Malia called after her, in full sergeant major mode.

Kamila left the room and stood underneath the spiral staircase outside. She took her mobile phone out of her handbag and tried to call Murad but there was no reply, so she left a message.

'Murad, where are you?' she began in a loud whisper. 'I'll kill you! Operation Rehab ends now! I'm *dying* here. I've been roped into dancing, and that too with some nerd from school. Siraj Khan. You probably don't remember him. I certainly didn't. This isn't funny! I'll *die* if I have to stay here a moment longer!'

She angrily tossed her phone into her bag and looked up to see Siraj Khan a few feet away from her. He had been dispatched to get some *dupattas* for the guys to wear around their necks during the dance. She felt a moment of panic and confusion as she had a dreadful feeling that he might have heard what she had said. He did not, however, seem to give any indication that he had and merely walked back into the lounge. Kamila followed after a moment or two.

'Finally!' said Malia when she saw Kamila walk into the room. 'Now take your places. Stand in a line. Your partners will stand behind you.'

Malia demonstrated and explained the routine and everyone followed her lead. There were lots of laughs as most people kept forgetting their steps; Malia and Ayyan bickered, Zaki and Adnan could not keep up; Lamia kept bumping into Kiran; only Siraj and Kamila seemed to be in sync. Much to her surprise, Kamila actually started enjoying herself. Even Laila, watching from one of the sofas, became part of the laughter.

After about an hour, the dance team stopped to take a break. Ayyan collapsed on the sofa; Lamia and Kiran went off into the dining room with Zaki and Adnan; Malia was called to inspect the fairy lights, while Siraj and Kamila went to get some water from the round table in the corner of the lounge.

'So, my reluctant partner didn't *die*!' said Siraj smiling as he poured some water in a glass for Kamila.

Kamila inwardly flinched. *He had heard!* How inconvenient.

'No. I didn't,' Kamila said, annoyed by the sheepishness in her voice. 'Actually, I don't like dancing.'

'Neither do I. But Malia can be very convincing,' Siraj said, laughing.

*If by convincing you mean bossy*, thought Kamila.

'So, what made you think that staying here a moment longer would lead to your certain death?' Siraj asked in good humour.

Kamila winced. 'Um. Nothing,' she said as she tried to think of an excuse. 'It's just that, well, none of my friends are here and…'

'And do your friends always have to be around for you to have a good time?'

'Well, yes...'

'So, you don't like meeting new people?'

*It depends on who they are.*

'I heard you're the editor of a magazine?' continued Siraj.

'The publisher. I own it.'

'That sounds great. Do you enjoy it?'

For some reason, the question irritated her. 'Well, it's easy,' she responded.

'So, you *don't* enjoy it?'

'I never said that!' replied Kamila annoyed. 'I just said it was easy.'

Siraj nodded thoughtfully.

'So, what do you enjoy? What are your hobbies?'

Kamila thought for a moment. 'Well, I'm very busy. I don't have much time for hobbies.'

'Busy with the magazine?'

'Yes. And… other stuff,' said Kamila feeling like she was under a microscope.

Malia's voice boomed through the room again: 'Okay, break's over! Come back! Nobody's leaving till this dance is perfect!'

'Uff! I want to go back to Lahore!'

'Ayyan, shut up! And don't step on my foot this time!'

Siraj rolled his eyes and smiled. 'Back to the grindstone.'

They started walking back when Kamila was accosted by Mrs. Bilal and taken aside, none too subtly.

'What's the matter?' Kamila whispered, irritated.

'I just got all the stats on Siraj Khan,' said Mrs. Bilal in an excited and loud whisper. 'He's a lawyer, works at some fancy law firm, lives in London, has a fabulous flat in Notting Hill, both his parents are dead…'

Kamila glowered at Mrs. Bilal. 'And why would I be interested in this?'

'My dear, he's so eligible! And Naheed told me that he's also very nice—kind, polite, good values—so that's a bonus!'

'Uh! Aunty, he was at school with me. He was one of the nerds.'

'Darling, it's the nerds that make the best husbands. Always marry the nerds!'

Kamila was appalled. This talk was vulgar.

'*Beta,* he may not be spindles and acres rich but he's from a respectable, educated family and he's hardworking. Lawyers make loads of money! And they have long working hours, another bonus!'

'Aunty, please keep your voice down or someone will hear you!'

'Kamila listen, the problem with girls like you is that you don't know how to fish! You think the fish will simply swim your way. They won't! Fish are dumb by nature. Remember that. They need to be baited!'

Kamila was aghast. If she were going to go fishing, she wouldn't cast her net at a lawyer. She hired lawyers! She didn't marry them!

'*Beta*, Siraj Khan's a catch! Don't let him swim away! I wanted him for Lamia but he's clearly not interested in her, she's too light-hearted and he's the serious type. You two are more suited. Now please, go and speak to him nicely. Don't frown. You look so pretty when you smile. I shall go into mourning if he doesn't marry one of my girls! And you are now one of my girls!'

'KAMILA!' yelled Malia. 'Hurry!'

Kamila virtually ran back to the dance practice, such was her relief at extricating herself from this conversation with Mrs Bilal. She quickly took her place next to Siraj in the dance formation. Just as they were beginning though, the MP3 player stopped working. An exasperated Malia charged towards it purposefully.

'I love reading,' Kamila said suddenly to Siraj. 'That's one of my hobbies. You asked earlier.'

'Oh!' he replied sounding interested. 'Who's your favourite author?'

Kamila thought for a moment.

'Well it may sound trite, but it's Jane Austen.'

'Oh! *Pride and Prejudice*!'

'Among others,' Kamila said, smiling. This time with genuine pleasure.

'Mr. Darcy!'

'Yes,' she replied wearily.

'Uff, you know!' interrupted Ayyan, overhearing their exchange, 'Mr. Darcy has done more to ruin marriages than any other man in history!'

This comment was met by audible horror from all the ladies present, all of whom started arguing with Ayyan; Lamia and Kiran started playfully hitting him with cushions.

'What? It's true!' cried Ayyan, revelling in the reaction he'd provoked.

'Ayyan, shut up!' said Malia, still plugging and unplugging things. 'What do you know about Mr Darcy? You've never read a book in your life.'

'I saw the movie,' he said. 'And all I've heard since I got married is, "Mr Darcy this, Mr Darcy that!" *Yaar* the guy's ruined it for the rest of us!'

The room erupted into animated discussion, with everyone talking heatedly at the same time about the merits and demerits of Ayyan's comments.

Siraj turned to Kamila. 'I think you've sparked a revolt!'

She laughed. Just then, she heard her phone buzz and walked over to the sofa to take it out of her handbag. There was a text message from Murad:

*'I'm on my way. And Siraj Khan's a hottie!'*

####

Everyone at the well-attended *mehndi* held in the Qasims' large garden concurred that Kamila Mughal was dazzling. Her clothes were elegant and she had danced beautifully with that lawyer from London.

Along with dancing, Kamila had cheerfully socialised with people she would have ordinarily looked down on; Siraj introduced her to some of his friends—they were jovial and warm. Everything was going well and then suddenly, just like that, it all went to pieces.

Faisal entered with Erum.

Kamila froze.

She heard lots of squealing as people rushed towards the newlyweds. From what she could make out, Faisal, knowing that Erum and Maryam were friends, had surprised Erum by flying them in his Gulfstream to Islamabad to make an unexpected appearance. They would stay until the wedding and then resume their honeymoon, this time in Santorini.

For a moment, Kamila and Faisal's eyes met. He gave her a slight nod and then continued to talk to the people around him. Kamila went inside as steadily as she could, resisting the urge to run.

Siraj came in looking for her and found her sitting at the foot of the stairs.

'Is everything alright?' he asked with some concern.

'Yes, thank you,' Kamila said, trying not to look flustered.

'Did something happen? Did someone say anything to upset you?' Siraj asked, sitting down beside her.

'No. I upset myself.'

'Not that this is any of my business,' Siraj said after a moment's reflection, 'but does this have anything do with Faisal Dayyan's appearance? You went kind of... funny once you saw him.'

'No!' replied Kamila firmly. She did not want to discuss this with him.

Siraj nodded as he struggled to find tactful words. 'It's just that—well—you kind of had a thing for him even at school.'

'A *thing*?' Kamila said, not sure whether to laugh or cry.

'He's your answer to Mr Darcy?' asked Siraj smiling.

'No!'

*Yes,* she thought.

'Come, let's go outside,' said Siraj. 'Everyone's on the dance floor. And even though, according to you, I was born on the wrong side of the tracks, I'd be honoured if you'd dance with me without wanting to *die* this time.'

Kamila burst out laughing.

The *mehndi* was now in full swing—people were dancing, others were enjoying the buffet, the Islamabad Aunties seemed to be having a great time, clearly in an ecstasy of judging everyone present. Murad had turned up and was standing in the courtyard near the tables with Laila.

Mrs Bilal rushed over to them. 'Mission accomplished!' she said breathlessly to a bewildered Laila. 'I think Siraj is hooked!' she added.

Laila rolled her eyes at Murad who didn't respond. She placed a teaspoon of *biryani* on her plate. 'I think I should get a divorce', she said. 'After all, I'm thirty-two and need to think about getting married again.' And then it was Murad's turn to roll his eyes.

###

Mrs Bilal was right. Two weeks after Maryam's wedding, Kamila left for her summer vacation to London and got in touch with Siraj. Discovering that London for

Kamila meant Knightsbridge or Sloane Street, Siraj took her to his favourite haunts and she found herself falling in love with the city in a whole other way. London wasn't the only thing she fell in love with.

A year later, they were married in an elegant ceremony at Chatsworth House.

'How is it that all the mean girls get the nice guys?' Erum Dayyan whispered to her sister Jahanara Mughal as they sat together at Kamila's wedding.

Laila got her divorce and in a turn of events that surprised everyone, most of all herself, she started her own home furnishing company, which eventually opened retail outlets in every major Pakistani city.

Kamila sold *Pink* shortly after her wedding. She decided to pursue her original dream of being an author. She was nervous as anything about how her book, *The Problem with Mr Darcy*, would be received but she needn't have been, as it sold truckloads of copies just as Siraj had told her it would, and landed a film deal.

Ayyan received special thanks in the acknowledgments and was thrilled to have his name mentioned. He even attempted to read it.

# The Autumn Ball

Gayathri Warnasuriya

*"To be fond of dancing was a certain step towards falling in love"*

—Pride and Prejudice

Maya longed to go to the ball.

The problem was Prince Charming, or at least Prince Charming-once-upon-a-time, her husband, Hugo, who'd developed an aversion to socialising in general and to dancing in particular.

It hadn't always been like this, they'd met at a club in London and gone out dancing on their first few dates. He wasn't the most romantic or expressive man she'd come across but Maya was drawn to his solid and quiet demeanour. Maya sensed he didn't say things unless he meant them. This was proven a few months later when he proposed, albeit rather prosaically. One evening at dinner, he asked her if she'd like to get married as he had been assigned his first posting in the Foreign Service and she could accompany him as his wife. He had not got down on one knee, he had not arranged a string quartet, he had not even bought a ring. It was much more practical, in Hugo's viewpoint, to buy a ring after Maya accepted. She did. She was thrilled to.

London was the centre of the world and she loved it, but she'd been living there ever since her family left Pakistan when she'd been nine. She was ready for a change. *London had its perks but it also ground one down*, she thought. So many of her friends were looking for work abroad for a better quality of life after all. She liked her job as a deputy editor at The Journal of Forensic Sciences but there would be other opportunities. She told Hugo the next day over dinner how she'd try to find a job at a science institute in Abuja. It would be a problem, Hugo said, as a 'trailing spouse', the wife of a diplomat, she wasn't allowed to work unless it was for a charity or the embassy. *That didn't sound too bad*, Maya thought, though it would be strange to not have her own salary. But with a science background, she could edit a journal for a charity, even brush up on her research skills. Besides, she thought, she wasn't going to complain about the opportunity to be a lady of leisure for once, by the side of a handsome and charming man whom she was going to spend her life with. Her family felt much the same way. While they had been hoping Maya would meet a nice Pakistani boy, when she had refused to be introduced to any more following a series of mortifying meet-ups and *rishtas* from distant cousins and sons of friends, they had accepted it. While it would take Maya further away from them, they were happy for her.

Hugo's first posting had been to Abuja, a new, purpose-built capital in the centre of Nigeria. They arrived as newlyweds and the first year of meeting people and exploring the country had seemed like an extended honeymoon. They sat outside at midnight, eating spicy roast Nile Perch at the city's ubiquitous fish bars, went to weekend parties at the British High Commissioner's Residence in Kaduna, and danced all night to Femi Kuti at the New Africa Shrine in Lagos. Maya felt relieved she didn't have a job because the diplomatic scene was so social, and Hugo so busy that it was a given that she would set up and run the house. It wasn't remotely unsatisfying, this is how she discovered the city, by sourcing things she needed for home. She went on a series of adventures during the day, and in the evening when Hugo came home, they would swap stories and guffaw at mishaps. Keen to be the perfect wife, Maya made a real effort to make friends among the diplomatic and expat community. They were both invited out a lot and she felt it her role to make sure everyone's hospitality was repaid beautifully in her home. Hugo would praise her dinners, her presentation, and her knack for making conversation with some fairly stodgy diplomats to the high heavens, and she would beam.

Two years into their posting, Maya found herself pregnant, which only added to her happiness. Her parents told her to come home to them for the birth but she didn't want to leave Hugo, and he'd promised to be as hands-on as his work hours allowed, which, it turned out, wasn't very much. *He had a hard job,* she thought, *he was always travelling within the country and meeting people and his colleagues spoke so highly of his work*. Besides, he'd take the baby off her hands for a few hours on weekends, unless Armaan was crying, in which case, he wouldn't know what to do and would return him promptly. *Still, they had staff,* she thought, *and she'd trained them well*. How much harder this would have been in London with her cooking and cleaning and running errands on top of it. The last year of their Nigeria posting passed in a blur of childminding, and before she knew it, Hugo was offered another post – Pakistan.

Life was nothing if not unexpected, she had never thought marriage would bring her back to the country she'd left during her childhood. While her parents had returned occasionally for weddings and funerals, money had been tight when they'd immigrated to England, and they'd not been able to take her home for holidays, much as she'd cried and pleaded. As time passed, they felt the country had changed beyond recognition and rather than home, it began to feel like a scary, violent foreign place which most of their relatives and friends had also chosen to leave. Going as Hugo's wife made her feel both excited and nervous. In England, she'd never quite shaken that feeling of being too Pakistani to be British. She wondered now if she was desi enough for Pakistan.

The leafy suburb of Islamabad she found herself living in with Hugo was very different to her childhood memories of Rawalpindi. There were no auto-rickshaws and snarls of traffic. No bazaars crammed with people and wares, and few street-side vendors selling *kulfi* and *chaat*. Islamabad's streets were virtually empty, wide, tree-lined and astonishingly clean compared with its twin city. The houses were large and palatial and property prices were the steepest in the country.

In the cosmopolitan echelons of the Pakistani elite and international expatriates, she was not entirely at ease. In Nigeria, she had clearly been a foreigner and an expat; in Islamabad, the lines were blurred. The city was a grid of alphabetical sectors and street numbers. At a weekend retreat in the Murree Hills, she'd heard someone joke about the sectors of Islamabad. 'E is for the elite, F is for the foreigners, G is for government, H is for hospitals, and I is for the idiots who think they're living in Islamabad but are actually living in Pindi,' a scion of the landowning aristocracy had drawled, for Rawalpindi, though adjacent to Islamabad, was a different version of urban Pakistan altogether, where anywhere other than Westridge was beyond the pale. Maya was acutely aware that where she had grown up was very much outside the bounds of fashionable society but she had guffawed along with everyone else for she lived in F-sector now. Her parents had told her about relatives that she had to visit and though her two cousins, several times removed, and their parents, had greeted her warmly, it was an afternoon tea of awkward silences as she absorbed their entirely different lifestyles and mentalities. She searched out school friends on Facebook and found two, most were lost to changed surnames. They too seemed to be from another world, more conservative, more traditional, more family-oriented, it seemed, from photos. She sent out messages and was warmly invited over by both – this was one aspect in which Pakistan never failed – but had yet to take up the invitations for fear of how little they'd have to say to each other.

Though she often felt like an impostor in Islamabad's high society, she was slowly getting accustomed to socialising with school-mum cliques from the American school, who met up for 8 am coffee mornings and pre-school-run lunches. There, they discussed their children, whom they then paired up for playdates, the new butcher or carpenter they'd discovered, or the private residence you could buy fresh cheese from in the mornings.

It was strange to treat Pakistan like a foreign country. A year in, she was getting used to it. It was all made easier by the many cocktail parties and diplomatic receptions which Maya loved. She'd enjoyed going out in Abuja too, but now with a young child and a busy husband, these felt like a lifeline – dressing up, feeling like a woman and not just a mother, and enjoying some grown-up company.

The Autumn Ball was *the* event of the Islamabad social calendar, a mishmash of international diplomats, do-gooders, and the generally well-heeled and well-connected. It wasn't a dinner or cocktails, it was a ball. Maya longed for an opportunity to dance. Her friend Marco had two spare seats at his table. She had said yes immediately but when she'd mentioned it to Hugo, he'd said 'we'll see', which she'd come to recognise meant 'no.' She didn't usually push him on things because recently, overwork had meant he could be rather short with her. This, however, mattered and she was going to bring it up again.

It was six the next evening when Maya returned from tea with other diplomats' wives at a restaurant with a rooftop terrace overlooking the Margalla Hills. She was surprised to find Hugo already home and sprawled on the living room sofa reading. 'Armaan's sleeping,' he said when he saw her, knowing her routine of heading first to his room. 'I've sent Khalida home.'

She sat down next to his feet where he'd stretched them out, waiting for him to ask her where she'd been, and perhaps, tell her she looked nice.

'How was your day?' she said finally, to his silence.

'Oh, you don't want to know!' he said, not putting down his book. 'There's a reception at the Romanian Embassy tomorrow so I'll be home late.'

'Hugo?'

'Hmmm.'

'I'd like to go to the ball. There are two seats at Marco's table and if we're not taking them, he'll need to find someone else', she said, anxiously.

'Oh God, I see these people every day, Maya,' he said, putting down his book so she could see him roll his eyes at her. 'Do I really have to pay for a seat and put on an uncomfortable tux to see them again? Don't we go to enough parties?'

'We do,' she said, wondering when she had become this person to whom going out mattered so much, 'but never to dance. Besides everyone will be there, and we haven't hosted a dinner in a few months now, and actually you don't see these people all the time.'

Hugo paused for a few moments, measuring his desire to not attend against her argument. 'Alright,' he said, grudgingly.

'Oh, Hugo, we'll have so much fun', Maya said, grinning broadly. 'You're always the handsomest person in any room in your tux, and…'

'I have to get to that reception, Maya,' Hugo said, ending the conversation.

Maya went upstairs, slightly deflated, but still excited at the idea of the ball. She flung open her cupboards and started sifting through her things. She needed a dress. She hadn't bought any recently because she hadn't needed any in Islamabad, where a dressy top with trousers was more appropriate evening wear.

Taking a few of her old dresses as a guide to styles, a length of chartreuse silk, and a few clippings from magazines, Maya headed to her tailor in the Blue Area. When she had first arrived in Islamabad, she had been amused by the rigid colour coding and demarcations of the city, so different to the organic sprawl of Pindi. The Red Zone encompassed most government buildings including the Parliament House and the Diplomatic Enclave containing foreign embassies. Queries from where to buy a kettle to how to unlock your phone were always met by a vague wave of the hand and the response 'Blue Area', a broad swathe of shops and restaurants running alongside the imposing Jinnah Avenue. With time, she had become fond of this area, having found many treasures within, a little cavern of a shop full of blue pottery from Multan, an Iranian restaurant with the best kebabs in the city, and her tailor, Riaz, who could make any kind of *kurta pajama* and replicate Western clothing, a claim she'd hence far only tested with a series of increasingly elaborate tops.

She discussed the dress with Riaz, the neckline (deep), the hem (low), the swing and flow of the skirt, and left nervous but hopeful. A week later when she returned to try it on, she was relieved to see that the tailor had not exaggerated his ability. It was a little on the tight side, though Riaz insisted that there was no miscalculation on his part but that she had become 'healthier', the local euphemism for 'overweight'. Maya was far too embarrassed to argue. Besides, even if it was a little more snug than she had envisioned, standing in the dress in front of her mirror at home, she felt voluptuous and more feminine than she'd felt in a long time. She asked Armaan, playing nearby, what he thought of it and he said she looked pretty, never mind that he also said that when she was standing in pyjamas flossing her teeth in the morning.

Hugo's tuxedo, retrieved from the dry cleaners, was brushed down and was looking as good as always. It fit him like a glove. She helped him with his cufflinks and told him that he looked like James Bond.

'You're very sweet,' Hugo said, brushing down his tuxedo one last time. She lingered, waiting for the return compliment, but when none came, she headed to Armaan's room to say an always heart-breaking goodbye.

As they drove to the Diplomatic Enclave, she turned the radio on. There was a hip-hop song playing sampling an Afrobeat track they used to listen to in their Nigeria days. 'Remember this, Hugo?' she said, nostalgic for the younger versions of themselves, bowling along dusty red roads listening to the same music. It felt like a long time ago. As a diplomat's wife, you had to be discreet but she'd spoken as delicately as possible with a female friend in Islamabad about how her marriage felt different after Armaan had been born. Her friend had said this was perfectly natural and that it would mature into something different but equally beautiful. Maya eagerly awaited that moment.

Night fell as they turned on to Constitution Avenue lined with the grand buildings of high office, still brilliantly decorated from the Eid ul Adha celebrations a week ago. The austere white marble was almost gaudy with looped green, red, and yellow fairy lights. It was the end of a long hot summer and would soon give way to crisp autumn skies and the wedding season. Despite Hugo's protestations of it being too hot to wear a tux, the air was cool and she was glad of the cashmere shawl draped around her bare shoulders.

A long line of cars snaked their way into the enclave, heading towards the parking area but Hugo took a turn and parked slightly further out. As Maya alighted from the car, she took care to hold the hem of her dress clear of the wild tangle of bushes that grew around the outer perimeter of the Mediterranean Club. Industrial hemp grew wild all over Islamabad, and the scent of it combined with the anticipation of the revelry made her feel lightheaded.

Inside, they found a simple white canopy, decorated with fairy lights, and a raised wooden platform for a dance floor. White pillars were tastefully swathed with ice blue LED lighting. The décor was pleasantly low-key, perhaps because all of the city's other decorations were still being used elsewhere.

They made their way to their table, stopping en route to greet Hugo's colleagues and assorted acquaintances. Some of Maya's friends from Armaan's school were virtually unrecognisable from their morning avatars, transformed tonight into soigné women with salon updos in a mix of cocktail and floor-length dresses.

In the excitement of getting two tickets for Marco's table, Maya had failed to find out who else would be on it. She realised with an inward groan that one of the guests would be Salma, Hugo's colleague and Principal Political Officer at the British High Commission. Salma's eyes lit up when she saw Hugo, but it might have been Maya's imagination that saw Salma's eyes narrowing when she beheld her.

'Hi Hugo, how lovely to see you!' she smiled seductively. 'Maya,' she added as an afterthought, 'what an unusual colour you're wearing.'

'Thank you, Salma,' Maya said, with a fake smile plastered on her face.

'It's not everyone who can carry off chartreuse,' Salma added with the sort of look that left Maya in little doubt that she couldn't.

'You look wonderfully sexy, darling. Welcome to the ball!' Marco said, air-kissing her hello. Maya smiled her thanks up at him. Marco was the chief-of-party of a reputable non-governmental organisation in Islamabad. He took his title very much to heart and was often at the forefront of planning and organising the most splendid out-of-hours soirées in the city.

Maya realised that Salma was at their table because her date for the night was one of Marco's colleagues, Andreas. Maya had met him before, he was nice enough, if rather staid. She suspected that he was there to hang on Salma's arm till someone with more polish came along, someone like Hugo with his public-school pedigree, for example.

Salma had been perfectly courteous towards Maya when they first met but her tone changed soon after Maya had told her about her childhood in Rawalpindi.

'Oh, your father was an electrician?' Salma had said, with the fascinated tone of one examining someone's skin disease.

'He ran an electrical contracting business, yes.'

From then on, any exchange with Salma was filtered, Maya felt, with a certain level of contempt for her background. It was clear to her that Salma didn't think Maya was good enough for Hugo, and that she, with a background of privilege and all the right connections, would have made a better choice.

Maya was diverted from these thoughts by the arrival of the other couples who completed their table. Shehryar and Javaria were both journalists and very much part of the young and trendy media set whom Maya found great company, even though Hugo didn't seem to feel the same way. Then there was Rizwan, no one really knew what Rizwan did, only that he was very rich and owned a lot of land. His wife, Aleena, was a fashion designer who brought out a line of increasingly bizarre clothes every season. Her latest 'pret collection' was a series of belted and bedazzled gauzy ponchos which could only be carried off by women with absolutely no hips or bums.

'You look fabulous, babe,' Aleena said, looking appreciatively at Maya through a cloud of vape smoke. 'Where did you find this gorgeous dress?'

'My tailor made it for me,' Maya admitted somewhat sheepishly. Aleena was sure to be wearing designer wear.

'Very impressive,' Aleena said, warmly, chatting about the coming season's necklines.

Maya cast a quick glance at Hugo, who was listening to Rizwan telling a long story, and already looking bored She understood that these were Marco's, and by extension, her friends and not his, but she wished he would make more of an effort to appear interested.

Just then a friend, Aneela, spotted her from across the room and came over to say hello. She was a rare acquaintance from her childhood days. Aneela's mother had known hers, and even though Aneela was much younger than her, she had sought Maya out when she had arrived in Islamabad. By coincidence, she was working at the British High Commission as an administrative assistant. She was with Adam, the new political officer. Maya thought them a sweet couple, but as they walked away, she heard Salma mutter to Javaria, 'I wonder how long that's going to last. Of course, he's her ticket out of here.'

Maya looked at her pointedly. Salma realised she'd overheard her, and in spite of her entrenched snobbery, blushed.

'I think dinner is served,' Salma said, sounding flustered. She stood up and walked towards the buffet table.

Hugo and Maya followed, finding the buffet an eclectic mix of dishes to reflect the international flavour of the event.

The music started as soon as dinner was cleared away. The DJ christened the evening with 'La Bamba'.

Yes, it was corny but it was lively, and everyone knew it, and she was itching to dance. With the exception of Mario and Rizwan, the music was received with coolness at their table. She saw Salma rolling her eyes. Maya couldn't bear another second in her company.

'Hugo, come on, let's dance,' Maya said, holding out her hand.

'To this? I don't think so!' he said.

Salma smirked.

'Well, I'd like to dance,' Maya said, looking at Hugo.

Marco swooped in, 'I should be honoured,' he said, taking her hand. She was furious with Hugo for showing her up in front of their table, especially in front of that awful woman. She looked at him and shrugged, and took Marco's hand.

She felt slightly self-conscious at first but soon forgot herself and began to dance. The music wasn't great, it was true, but everyone around her seemed to be having a great time and she was determined to be part of the revelry, with or without her husband.

Nobody had told her that marriage would be so lonely.

Even in the cool evening, it was warm under the canopy, thanks to the gyrating bodies and the wine. After some spirited moves to 'Girls Just Wanna Have Fun,' Maya went to get a drink of water. She also sensed the approach of the more maudlin segment of the evening as the DJ was beginning to veer towards 'slow dance numbers', and she thought it best to get off the dance floor. On her way to the bar, she spotted Hugo talking to a random diplomat though the conversation appeared stilted, and Hugo had his fake politely-interested face on. She walked up to them.

'I am sorry to interrupt but I am just about to commandeer my husband onto the dance floor,' Maya said with a charming smile. The random diplomat smiled and bid them good night.

'Come on, let's dance,' she smiled up at Hugo.

'Maya, I really don't feel like dancing. The music is terrible. I'm bored and I'd really like to go home. It's almost midnight anyway. Khalida's husband will pick her up soon. We should just go home.'

She thought of when he had first met her when he had begged her to dance with him. He hadn't been quite so particular about the music then.

'Yeah, let's go,' she said, turning her head away. She was close to tears.

No one was at the table as everyone had drifted off to mingle or to dance so they quickly went outside and got into their car, which Hugo had parked in the tangle of hemp, prepared for a quick getaway.

As Hugo drove back along Constitution Avenue, she sat next to him in stony silence.

'Look, I'm sorry I didn't dance but I…' he began, but the sudden violent sobbing that emanated from his wife stopped him in his tracks.

'This isn't working,' she said, 'we're just a joint parenting unit.'

'Maya, I think you are overreacting. I...'

'No, I'm not. I looked forward to this night for so long and you made no effort to dance or even pretend that you're enjoying yourself. Would it have killed you to look happy for one moment?' she said, crying more out of anger than disappointment.

'You seemed to be having a great time with your mates. I walked around and chatted with some guys from work. I kept waiting for a decent song to come on but it never did. I think you're blowing this way out of proportion, but all the street lights are off and I really need to focus on the road. Can we please talk about this when we get home?' Hugo said and they completed the rest of the journey in silence punctuated by the sound of Maya sniffling.

The front door opened as soon as the car drove up the driveway. Khalida stood at the door with Armaan in her arms.

'Madam, Armaan woke up half an hour ago and is crying too much for his mama. He doesn't want to sleep again,' Khalida said.

Armaan reached out for Maya, his face puckered up in tears. She gave him a cuddle but had to pay Khalida whose husband was waiting on his motorbike, so she passed her son to Hugo who took him upstairs to his room.

'Madam, why are you sad?' asked the woman who probably knew her better than anyone else in Islamabad.

'I am OK, Khalida, just a little tired. Thanks very much and good night. Get home safe,' Maya said as she locked and bolted the front door.

Walking upstairs to Armaan's room, she looked in to find Hugo asleep on Armaan's bed with Armaan fast asleep in his arms. The room was warm and the curls were pasted down on both their foreheads. Maya felt an overwhelming surge of love. Hugo was a good dad, a great dad. Perhaps she *had* overreacted. She wasn't sure what she wanted to do, it was all so much more complicated than she thought marriage would be.

Maya walked out onto the balcony. The Margalla Hills were outlined in the distance. There was a power cut and the generator hummed below, but did not drown out the sound of music coming from the park in front of their house. A few youngsters had parked their cars on the pavement and were talking, laughing, and playing dance music on their car radios as loud as they could. It sounded like pop with a hip-hop beat and even though she didn't know the song, she began to slowly dance alone.

# Only The Deepest Love

## Sonya Rehman

*"The more I see of the world, the more I am dissatisfied with it"*

—Pride and Prejudice

'Samina? I need to see you, can we meet?' Sobia's voice was shaky.

'Are you alright?' I asked, panicking slightly.

'Not really, when do you get off from work?'

'3 pm tops, at The Deli?'

It had to be that husband of hers; something about him didn't sit well with me, though it had been an arranged marriage and I barely knew him. I had only had a chance to observe him at the wedding last weekend as he sat there looking regal in his gold sherwani with a crimson pagri perched on his head, Sobia sitting stiffly next to him in an elaborate tea-pink and gold ensemble, weighed down by kundan and gold. Perhaps he was just nervous or maybe it's in his nature to be reserved, but you didn't feel any real warmth from him for any of us or even really for Sobia. Still, I didn't want to judge anyone on a meeting at such a stressful time. Maybe this was the male version of Bridezilla. Also, the idea of my dear sweet cousin, who was the closest thing I had to a sibling, having married someone cold was something best banished from the mind.

What could possibly have happened in a week? Surely they were still just getting over the fatigue of having entertained half of Lahore?

The memory of the wedding brought a blush to my cheeks. In a mortifying moment I'd tripped over my Chantilly lace sari and bumped into a waiter carrying a plate of canapés that had then landed on me. I would have ended up on the floor if some friend of Asad's hadn't steadied me just in time. Unfortunately, the steadying had involved him holding me rather intimately, if only for a few seconds. What a way to be introduced. God, I hope I never have to relive the embarrassment by bumping into him again!

I didn't get the time to think about any of it for the rest of the day as my schedule was so heavy this semester that I had to half-jog towards my undergrad class a few blocks away from my office to make it on time.

The weather was beautiful – a light breeze and and a grey, overcast sky thick with clouds. Lahore lapped up the last dregs of the monsoons before the onset of winter.

I'd been at the Lahore School of Media Studies for two years now and though it was hard work I loved it. Teaching hadn't always been the plan, I'd had some rather grand hopes about hosting an art and culture show for television. But then came a combination of me not making the cut and also the revelation that people who watch TV aren't actually that interested in the arts.

Initially I'd hated the long commute to the suburbs. Chocolate brown cows and lethargic buffaloes grazed in fields broken up by the enormous farmhouses of Lahore's new money.

I was three minutes late to class. Opening the large whitewashed door set in a red brick exterior, the room was loud and noisy – clearly in overdrive. Asfandyar was intently watching me enter, his face flushed.

Last week I'd asked the batch of thirty-three to write a few paragraphs about something that inspired them: a scene, a memory – anything, to prepare them for a bigger feature writing assignment before their mid-terms. He'd handed in a few scrawled lines, barely coherent, reflecting a complete lack of effort. I'd given him a D.

He was giving me the stink-eye while I took attendance and immediately after, sauntered over, crackling in a very starched white shalwar kameez.

'Ma'am?' he said, waving his assignment in my face. 'Ma'am this is a *really* bad grade. I didn't deserve this.'

'I think I was quite generous given your work.'

'That's not fair ma'am, I think I deserved a better grade.'

*Should I also award you a Pulitzer while I'm at it?*

I'd always had trouble with him. His father, Mian Khurshid Chaudhry, a landlord and politician who had recently joined the ruling political party as an MNA didn't have the cleanest reputation in town. Only a few months ago, one of his close associates had been accused of the rape of a girl who had gone missing a week after the news broke. But as was the case with most sordid scandals involving powerful perpetrators and powerless victims, news outlets conveniently forgot the story soon after.

'Asfandyar,' I said, 'Your handwriting was unreadable, and the content suggested that you hadn't been following the classes at all.'

I looked down at the attendance register signalling the end of our tête-à-tête.

'Ma'am?' he said, coming closer, looking me straight in the eye. 'Do you know *whom* my father is?'

I sucked in my breath and held his gaze, taking in his unibrow, the landscape of his cheeks covered in a mountain range of pimples, speckled with dots of pus.

'Whom? *Who*, you mean. You're not being graded on who your father is, Asfandyar – back to your seat now,' I said, looking down again.

Asfandyar sputtered with rage and marched out of the classroom, banging the door on his way out to an assortment of gasps from the class.

He's not welcome in this class ever again, I thought. 'Show's over' I said, trying to start the class after the dramatic distraction, as I started rigging the laptop up to the projector, partly to distract myself from the fact that I was, for all my bravado, scared.

No point worrying, I thought. I'll speak to the university administration when I get a chance.

'Ok class', I said, as cheerfully as I could manage, 'I've got something interesting to discuss with you today!' lining up the sickening clip of a TV anchor raiding a park looking for young people trying to hook up, as is normal and healthy. There'll be no shortage of things to discuss in class today!

###

Sobia was sitting upstairs in a corner at The Deli. She was hunched over, typing something out on her phone with a look of great concentration on her face.

'I almost didn't recognise you without the five pounds of jewellery.' I said, smiling.

Sobia jumped up and gave me a tight hug.

'Okay woman, what the hell is going on? You had me worried on the phone.' I flagged down a waiter and we got ordering out of the way. 'Now,' I said, taking a quick look at the largely empty tables around us to make sure we had sufficient privacy, 'Talk.'

She steepled her fingers and looked at me, clearly dreading the conversation. Dressed in skinny white jeans, and an apple green kurta with a gold choker against her pale skin, she looked almost adolescent for a twenty-four-year-old.

'Please don't share what I'm about to tell you with anyone, okay?' she said.

'Stop it,' I said. 'You know I won't, what happened?' I asked, holding her hand.

She picked up a saltshaker and twisted it in her fingers nervously.

'Here's the thing, when Asad and I made our way back to our hotel room after the ceremony, it didn't go as I thought it would...'

'What do you mean, exactly?' I said, with a fairly decent idea of what she meant.

She gulped and fidgeted in her chair. 'Once we were in bed, he turned over and that was that.'

'What did you do? Did you say anything?'

'Well, yes, I mean I hadn't bought a truckload of Victoria's Secret lingerie from Dubai for nothing,' she laughed uneasily before continuing. 'I stroked his back and kissed the side of his cheek. He didn't move. I thought he was tired, you know how crazy the wedding was.'

I nodded, thinking if he'd been tired on that one night, Sobia wouldn't be sitting here right now, a week later, telling me about it.

'But then the next night, and the night after that...'

'Same thing?' I asked.

She nodded.

'I was furious. I felt dismissed and rejected. This wasn't the way I'd imagined marriage to be.'

Tears began rolling down her face, I handed her a napkin. She blew her nose loudly.

'I mean I'd waited for this my whole life,' she said, 'Always played it safe, made sure I never dated even though my friends jumped from relationship to relationship. I saved myself knowing I was going to give myself to my husband – that's the way we've been raised, haven't we, Sam?'

Pained, I remembered Ameer, his stupid mushroom haircut and how he'd shattered my heart into a million pathetic pieces when I was Sobia's age.

I reached forward and held my cousin's hand. 'I'm so sorry Sobz, but we can sit here and make a thousand assumptions, but… look it's only been a week, – give it a little time. Who knows what's going on with him, maybe it's just something that needs an adjustment period.'

Alarm bells were clanging loudly in my mind but I tried to believe the words coming out of my mouth. Even before Sobia came to me with this awful revelation, I'd had my concerns.

'Sam, it gets worse,' she said. 'Last night, I was crying in bed as quietly as I could, I thought he'd gone to sleep. He got up and told me to get on my knees. I was so pathetically grateful even for this… so I got on my knees and then, nothing, the bastard dry humped me with his shorts on. Then he went for a shower, came back to bed and fell asleep within ten minutes.'

I held Sobia's hand tightly. I had no words, just suspicions that I didn't dare to verbalise.

'He doesn't think I'm attractive' Sobia said, crying again. 'Do you think he's in love with someone else? I wonder who she is.'

Or *he*, I thought, not wanting to introduce the possibility I strongly suspected.

The scenario was all too common. Being gay carried such a stigma that even if parents allowed themselves to suspect such a thing of their child, their 'solution' was marriage, to hell with their lives and the lives of the poor women who never got their chance at love.

My colleague Nafisa had gone through this. Her husband refused to consummate the marriage a good six months into their newlywed life. And even when they did it, it was forced, brief and impersonal. He never desired her.

It took Nafisa three years to figure out her husband swung the other way, and that too, by chance, when she stumbled on multiple gay porn websites bookmarked in her husband's laptop. Given their conventional upbringing, and the fact that the couple had two young children, divorce wasn't even an option.

'Don't think like that, Sobia, you know you're a beautiful girl – you've had scores of proposals. You chose Asad. Now listen, you monitor this, take it a day at a time, okay?'

She nodded, twisting the colossal rock on her finger round and round.

What lame advice I was shovelling out to my baby cousin. But what more could I have said? File for a divorce just days into her marriage? Or in her case, an annulment?

I was grateful for a hiatus in the conversation when the waiter arrived, bringing coffee, Caesar salad and late lunch of spicy Penne Arrabiata for me. It was a quarter past three and I swooped down gratefully on my pasta. 'Oh by the way,' Sobia said, sipping her coffee, 'Asad said his friend Hashim thought you were cute.'

With a forkful of pasta in my mouth, I half-choked, remembering the man who broke my fall at the wedding and blushing all over again.

###

Mum was in the kitchen peeling a head of garlic when I got home. Her movements were slow and deliberate. I noticed for the first time that her wavy salt and pepper coloured hair was thinning from the top. I was finally beginning to accept that she was getting older and more vulnerable, that I was becoming the parent in many ways. It was a complicated thing, sometimes I resented her for needing me so much. I'd helped keep the household afloat since she walked out on my father. I'd never say it but sometimes I even blamed her for leaving him, though most of the time, I was angry that she'd spent so much time in an abusive marriage with the man.

I kissed her cheek.

'Your father's sent you a package,' she said, pointing to the door with her knife.

I picked up the thick DHL envelope lying on a side table in the living room. Looking over my father's UK return address at the back of the package,

I ripped it open and pulled out a belated birthday card and a book of poetry by Nayyirah Waheed; *Salt*.

The card featured two white kittens playing with a ball of wool.

How odd, I'd thought, my father knew I hated cats. But at least he remembered I loved poetry.

Flipping it open, there in the large, loopy handwriting of a self-absorbed man, were my father's words:

*Dear Sam,*
*Apologies for sending this to you so late but I just returned from a trip to Scotland with the Mrs. Had a dogsitter look after Fifi and Max. Anyway, Happy 33rd, kiddo! Come visit us sometime.*
*Papa.*

Yeah, you fucker, like I can muster up a lakh on a teacher's salary to fly out to see you, I thought bitterly.

A picture of him and Rebecca slipped out from the card from their holiday. In it he looked fit, his arms toned and his skin glowing with a golden tan. He had a head full of thick white hair, his left cheek with that familiar, handsome dimple. He was a picture of contentment and had his arm draped over his young English wife's shoulders. She was wearing a canary yellow tea dress and had been photographed in the process of tucking a strand of blonde hair behind her ear. They both looked like they were laughing at some big, grand joke, in unison. Sparkly teeth, sunny first-world happiness.

It felt insulting and made me feel poor.

They'd met when my father had been working as a hotshot editor of a popular bi-monthly publication on current affairs, News Link. Rebecca had taken a trip to Pakistan to intern as a reporter and experience 'exotic' Pakistan while she was at it. They'd fallen in love in the newsroom during daylight hours while my father beat my mother black and blue in the evenings. I don't think my mother would've had the courage to leave him if she hadn't discovered his affair.

I touched my father's face with my thumb, hoping to rake up the last few dregs of love in my heart for him. But there was no trace of me in his shiny eyes, or of the life he had in Pakistan.

I ripped up the photograph and threw it in the bin.

###

Sanober, the accounts manager, had delayed my paycheque as usual. Since he was avoiding my calls, as was the norm in the accounts department, I walked over to their office to give him a piece of my mind one quiet afternoon when I'd stayed back late to catch up with some marking. I was walking back when I saw Asfandyar, gelled hair and glimmering Rolex, glaring at me. Looking away, I upped my pace towards the car park at the opposite end of the college compound. I glanced as casually as I could manage over my shoulder. He was still there, walking about eight feet behind me.

I looked towards the exit gate in search of Khan Baba, our trusted security guard who was nowhere to be seen.

I had at least spotted my car, I rummaged in my satchel for my key trying not to panic, listening to the sound of gravel crunching beneath my sandals.

I felt a firm grip on my shoulder. Before I could turn around, I was shoved against my car door. Hitting my head on the window, I slumped to the ground.

Looking up, my vision was filled with Asfandyar towering over me, his mouth twisted in a snarl.

'Don't you ever insult me like that again, you piece of shit!'

With that, he brought his boot down into the side of my ribs.

The pain was jagged and forceful; I buckled over, convulsing.

'Never forget your place, you *NOBODY*,' he screamed, 'I can have you picked up, raped and torn limb from limb!' With that, he spat on me, delivering another blow to my shoulder.

His eyes, blazing black with hatred, reminded me of Papa barging through the house breaking vases, plates, my mother's crystal decoration pieces; flinging them at my mother as she cowered over me, protecting me from the blows that followed.

All of a sudden I heard a scuffle break out; men were shouting profanities in Urdu and Punjabi,

Asfandyar yelled and then came the sound of a sickening crunch. Warm blood trickled in a sliver down from a wound near my scalp and into a tiny pool in my ear. I felt fingers gently wipe my forehead as I winced.

'God no, it's you. We have to stop meeting like this.'

Hashim held me, lifting me up carefully. A sharp pain shot across my ribcage as I tried to take a deep breath, now totally disoriented. Was I hallucinating? What was the man from Sobia's wedding doing rescuing me in a parking lot?

'Listen, let me carry you to my car, we need to get you to a doctor.'

'No no, I'll walk, don't worry,' I said quickly, suddenly conscious of my weight, of all ridiculous things.

I took mincing steps to his Civic and collapsed into the passenger seat. He turned and looked at me with an expression that made me feel sheer relief.

'Wait, what are *you* doing here?' I asked

'The Dean hired me last week as a visiting faculty member for their postgrad programme. I came to sign the contract today.'

'Are you serious?'

'I'm serious,' he looked over at me smiling, 'I decided to quit working for Lahore Beat,' he said, referring to a local news channel, 'Tried to catch up with you when you left the accounts office but you were sprinting away,' he paused, grinning. 'Anyway enough of that, where does it hurt? Don't worry, we're getting you to a doctor right now.'

With that he revved the engine and pulled out of the parking lot before I could say a word.

###

I woke at noon the next day.

Hashim had taken me home after we left the closest hospital to the campus and escorted me into the house where my mother feverishly ran to and from her bedroom checking on me and arranging extra pillows to prop me up on. Lying flat was painful.

Luckily I just had some cuts and bruises. I was prescribed a few strong painkillers.

Wincing, I turned over and checked my phone, remembering Hashim's face as he'd spoken to my mother at the front door on his way out. I was in pain and in shock from the trauma but I couldn't help but notice how handsome Hashim was.

My phone beeped.

*Samina, hope you're feeling better. You'd be pleased to know that the Dean expelled Asfandyar this morning. Not that he was on campus. They're registering an FIR against him at the police station.*

I typed out a response and added two smiley faces but then quickly deleted it. It felt silly. I decided to respond later with a clearer head.

In his WhatsApp display picture, Hashim had his glasses propped up on his head and was squinting and smiling at a little boy in his arms. Dressed in a white onesie printed with little blue ships and anchors, the toddler had a fist full of Hashim's right cheek in his chubby hand and was grinning a toothless baby grin back at Hashim.

That child *had* to be Hashim's nephew, or a friend's son, I reasoned. I mean, he'd hardly go about telling Sobia he thought I was cute if he was the married father of a newborn. Right? I pressed to the edges of my consciousness the things I knew men were capable of. Turning over, I pulled the duvet over my head and closed my eyes. The room was deliciously cool as I drifted into a deep sleep.

###

Two weeks after the incident, I walked into campus and was met by the Dean, my students and a stream of anxious colleagues. The Dean approved my request to be excused for the remaining duration of the term.

Asfandyar was in hiding.

There was talk that he'd fled to Dubai. A lawyer appointed by the college was aggressively pursuing the case. It was getting a fair amount of media attention. The hashtag #Jail4Asfandyar had been trending on Twitter.

Since the attack, Hashim came to see me every second day. There was a hint of winter in the air. Over cups of tea, conversation was easy and silences were comforting. I found out that he loved graphic novels, had backpacked through Europe when he was eighteen, and that he was divorced. He'd fallen in love with his college sweetheart and married her soon after graduating from Cambridge. They had a son, Hamza, now four. When I probed further one evening about how often he saw his son, Hashim fell silent and then swiftly changed the topic. I made sure never to bring it up again.

Some evenings, when Hashim couldn't drop by, he'd call instead, and we'd talk through the night – sharing silly details of our lives till daybreak when the call for Fajr prayers rang through a languid city.

At times I couldn't understand Hashim's interest in me and wouldn't return his phone calls or messages. I couldn't wrap my head around the fact that someone other than my mother thought I was nice to be around.

I was falling for him. It felt steady and warm.

Letting my guard down felt good. But at the same time I felt exposed and vulnerable. Every stupid love song reminded me of Hashim – his brown eyes, his neatly cropped beard, and most of all, his attentiveness.

But just as magically as it had started out, Hashim disappeared, almost as if he had never existed. An excrutiating week went by. Then two.

Not one to chase a man, I called Hashim twice and even sent him a few WhatsApp messages – I tried to keep it cool, not frantic. Nothing. No response. Had he gotten back together with his wife? Was it something I had done, said? I was a wreck. But why was I surprised? Didn't they always leave?

In the third week of Hashim's radio silence, my phone beeped with a message from Sobia. I was terribly disappointed it wasn't Hashim.

*Sam,*
*I miss you! I know you've been home for days in your PJs being a bum (Aunty tells me everything, btw), so get off that ass and come visit Asad and me in Nathiagali for a few days – the weather here is beautiful, misty evenings and all that! Please come!!*

*Love you,*
*Sobz.*
*xoxo*

###

She came dashing down the patio of her picturesque, one-storey holiday home as soon as she saw my cab pull into the long, S-shaped driveway.

Dressed in faded blue jeans and a snug red cashmere sweater with her hair in a messy bun, my cousin shrieked as I stepped out of the car, a tad disheveled, my grey hoodie pulled over my head.

Paying off the driver, I fell into Sobia's welcoming, bony arms. If my cousin had a spirit animal, it would have to be a friendly, glossy Labrador.

'Oh I'm so happy you made it, Sam! I thought you'd never snap out of hermit mode! God! Okay listen, Asad's in the kitchen whipping up some lunch for all of us,' Sobia said, linking her arm in mine as her guard carried my oversized knapsack and satchel into the house.

'Hashim got here a few hours ago by the way; I thought you guys were going to come together?'

*Hashim?* I felt pinpricks of excitement at the thought of seeing him, or was it dread? How embarrassing, would he have come if he knew I'd be here? I quickly told Sobia something along the lines of staying back to meet the deadline for a doctorate school application. Which, in a way, wasn't far from the truth. Since Hashim's disappearance, I'd decided to apply for a PhD program overseas.

Chatting away, Sobia whisked me into their expansive living room complete with Persian carpets, deliciously creaky wooden floors, large windows overlooking the mountains, and a huge floor to ceiling bookshelf lined with books on art, fiction, history and little artsy trinkets aesthetically placed on top and in between.

I plonked myself down on a beige leather sofa with a Sindhi print throw, Sobia ran off into the kitchen to get me a mug of hot chocolate.

'Hiiiii!' Asad blazed into the room with a wooden spatula in his hand. Wearing a black apron over khaki pants and a cream-coloured turtleneck, the glittering print on his apron read *Kiss The Cook!!* with two exclamation marks.

'Sobia's been fretting all day, Sam,' Asad said jovially, like an Aunt jokingly complaining about her silly daughter, 'She was like oh my God oh my God oh my Goddddd, Sam's sooooooo not going to make it! But I was like tsk tsk, don't be stupid jaanu, of course she will! And look! Here you are!' With that Asad did a little twirl, waving his spatula in the air like a wand.

I laughed and gave him a high five, visibly taken aback. His energy was infectious and sparkly – a far cry from Mr. Snorefest on his wedding day.

Motioning with his spatula to follow him into the kitchen, I perched on a chalky white stool as Sobia placed a steaming mug of hot chocolate on the counter before me. In it, miniature marshmallows floated about. It was delicious and hazlenutty.

As Asad and Sobia chatted with me animatedly while chopping onions, selecting spices and placing a pot of rice on the fire, I couldn't help but notice how they got along like school BFFs. Even when I tried to catch Sobia's eye, a quizzical expression secretly hidden in my expression only for her, she didn't take the bait.

I decided then not to snoop and just enjoy their company and the strange niceness of the situation I was in.

But when Asad excused himself from the kitchen to go to the loo, I finally had my chance and pounced on my cousin.

'Sobia, what the hell is going on? He's gay isn't he, and you know it!'

My voice, I realized, was verging on the hysterical.

'Yes, I know,' Sobia said softly as she carefully sliced through freshly washed coriander and green chillies. She didn't look up at me as she spoke.

'I'm giving it some time,' she said, weighing her words, 'I don't know what to do right now, I was thinking I may...well, we get along so well...'

Hashim strode into the kitchen, with Asad following closely behind. Hashim's eyes met mine briefly.

'Hashim! I was just going to call you over to join us! I'm so glad Asad fetched you! Did you have a nice nap?' Sobia said, her tone a pitch too high, 'I'm um, just going to get something from the garden for the chicken, Asad's planted a whole row of organic tomatoes! Asad, can you come give me a hand?'

Before waiting for an answer, Sobia grabbed him by the arm as they practically ran out the door.

'What's up with them?' I laughed awkwardly.

I couldn't hold his gaze for long and looked away, putting the yellow mug to my nose and then quickly taking a scorching sip.

Pulling up a stool next to mine, Hashim looked ahead while nervously adjusting the collar of his black corduroy jacket. He cleared his throat.

And right then, I felt the same, familiar sensation of resentment bubble up into my chest, rapidly making its way into my throat.

'Was it something I said? Or did?' I sputtered, unable to control my hurt and rage.

Tears sprang in my eyes as I tightened my fingers around the mug handle. I wanted to break it off and fling it into his poker face.

I knew what was coming, some half-arsed excuse. Then the rejection.

Placing my mug on the counter, I quickly got up. My emotions were feral and I didn't want to make a greater fool of myself.

Hashim continued to look ahead, his face tense, controlled.

And then, I was almost immediately enveloped by arms; my face against a warm chest, a heartbeat.

'I'm sorry,' he whispered in my ear, 'I just needed to think. I was scared too.'

As the afternoon mist rolled in, as Sobia and Asad's footsteps got louder in the hallway, and in the warmth of his embrace, I thought of a poem in the book that Papa had sent me and smiled.

# On the Verge

## Laaleen Sukhera

*"One cannot be always laughing at a man without now and then stumbling on something witty"*

—Pride and Prejudice

Three months ago, if you'd told me that I'd be spending my wedding night meeting a blind date, I'd have laughed. I'm not laughing now.

My love life could've passed for an indie film, one cast for diversity. The kind that starts out with a quirky situation, continues with a dose of hope, and concludes with an ambiguous ending. It'd be rated PG-13, limited to kissing and some mild expletives.

The storyline would go something like this: A reasonably accomplished, fairly attractive heroine with a functioning uterus experiences the downside of approaching thirty, with a fledgling career, no baby, no savings, and no man.

One magical evening, the heroine encounters a dashing prince who spurns his legion of admirers and proposes marriage to the endearing heroine after a whirlwind courtship.

Plot twist: In the midst of her Big Fat Pakistani Wedding preparations, the heroine discovers that there are other women in her prince's life. And so, to his utter disbelief, and slightly to hers, she calls off their splashy wedding and goes sailing into the sunset, solo.

End credits roll to emo song.

OK, so the actual ending was a little different. I was left to the mercy of the fickle Pakistani *beau monde* and greeted with inquisitive questions, snide remarks, and cruel snickers. I was handed a box of Xanax by well-meaning matrons and a *taveez* by my masseuse to ward off the envious eyes that undoubtedly caused my fiancé's errant ways. I was advised to lose a few more kilos, as if my slight love handles were to blame. 'One can *never* be too thin,' hissed a fashion designer acquaintance at a soirée.

'Good riddance,' said Ayana, my BFF, who'd been amazing as usual through all this. 'Can you imagine how awful it'd have been if you woke up two babies later and discovered him cheating then? You were *lucky*, Roya!'

'I sure don't feel lucky,' I muttered. She gave me a hug.

'Look, I'd tell you to get on Coffee Meets Bagel but it's Lahore. You know that Tinder account I made in London over the holidays? Well, when I logged back in here, it showed up my cook and my driver. I had to swipe Dildar and Razakat!'

We screamed with laughter.

Over many girls' nights over drinks and take-out, my friends and I vented, soul-searched, analysed, and overshared until we ran out of stories and theories, and I felt almost normal again. I'd been worried about my work; as a blogger, I'd had to rely on my own incentive to set deadlines and get things done, and I'd just not been up to it since things went south with Princey. I felt even more awful because I was losing the followers, the momentum, and the advertising I'd managed to get when I'd been doing regular posts about planning my wedding to a proper B-list celebrity. Some of Princey's friends had been the absolute height of tack, and while I never named them, a few of their more ostentatious flourishes made for great copy. I wasn't sure if anyone would be interested—after months of designer togs and nightclub interiors with Princey's flashy posse—in my current state—pyjamas, greasy hair, and Netflix. I needed to cover a splashy event to shake things up, to not be Sad Single Roya.

My Fairy Godmother came in the form of Sweetie Aunty, a friend of my mother's. She literally got me invited to a ball, and in the English countryside! Sweetie Aunty was a society doyenne, always in the right place at the right time, knew everyone, and was invited to everything. Not just here in Lahore, but around the world, wherever desi society congregated. *I knew another prince would come my way*, I thought, trying not to get too excited about it. 'Avondon Ball would be great for my blog,' I said.

'Blog?' Sweetie Aunty said in disgust. 'Do you know what Saqnain Tanvir is set to inherit?' she said, as we settled in her drawing room for a cup of Nespresso. Her tea trolley groaned with carblicious treats which neither of us dared touch.

'They have only just started moving properly in society in the last few years, ever since his father literally made a *killing* with their halal burger franchise in England. He went from Jameel Tanvir Butt of Gujranwala to Sir Jimmy Tanvir of Surrey. I'd promised your mother I wouldn't rest until I had settled you with a well-to-do, *khaata peeta* family. Chances like this don't come every day. If you wait any longer, you'll only have those awful divorced men with three children and three double chins left to choose from.'

I had to admit that the thought of meeting a man with three chins wasn't very tempting.

'He doesn't look very tall in his pictures' I said, a little doubtfully, looking him up on my phone as we spoke. 'I've always wanted to look up into a man's eyes, not have him look straight into my chest...'

'Don't be so naïve, *beta*! Stop Googling him, look for Avondon, their Surrey estate. They've filmed BBC dramas and Shah Rukh Khan movies there. He's having a *ball* to celebrate his 30th birthday! Imagine how grand-shand he is! So, what is an inch or two here and there with a house like that? You're a lovely girl, Roya *beta*, but do you know how many girls with decent backgrounds, anorexia, and designer clothes are waiting to pounce on him?'

Stopping for a sip of coffee, she continued, 'Men look at your chest whether it's at their eye level or not. These things are not important in the long run. Look what happened to your poor sister! *Bechari* Myra, still single at thirty-five and working like a drudge, refusing to let me find her anyone.'

Myra had decided to pursue a career early in life and barely got the time to meet men, plus she had almost no patience for fools, which was the commodity largely on offer. She'd been engaged once in her early 20s but that hadn't worked out, and after that she'd poured herself into caring for our mother who'd raised us alone since our father's death many years earlier. They'd both insisted that I not drop my degree halfway. I'd come back from Boston straight after though, we'd both looked after her till the end. Myra would go to her Corporate Communications job in the day and be with our mother in the evenings. I started blogging because the timings were totally flexible and because expressing myself helped me through this horrible time. When my mother died, it felt like our lives were over. Numb, we moved into a smaller flat, largely funded by Myra, and tried to make our lives feel like they mattered again.

Two weeks after meeting Sweetie Aunty, I was packing while Myra watched me with faint disapproval clouding her face.

'I'm just worried about you,' she said. 'Tell me you're OK?'

'Yes, I promise. I'm giving it my best shot or Sweetie Aunty will slaughter me!'

'Are you sure you aren't running away from your feelings about Princey?' Myra persisted. 'Do you really need to meet someone new this fast? It's only been a few months since you were engaged.'

'I'm not going to meet someone', I lied, 'I'm going because this is a great work opportunity for me.' *Plus, what's wrong with a nice, single millionaire, Myra?*

Myra hmmmed. She hadn't trusted Princey's bedazzled lifestyle either.

My phone beeped.

*'Can't wait to meet you!'*

It was him again! He'd been texting me regularly since Sweetie Aunty told him about me, he was so much warmer than I'd hoped. I blushed with pleasure each time he got in touch. It helped that I'd found a mention of him in one of my favourite gossip websites.

**The DailyTale**

- **Avondon Park is let at last! Developer Scott Tanvir, the son of Sir Jimmy Tanvir of Halal Burgerland, purchased the 12-acre Surrey property from Lady Avondon in 2015**
- **After a £4 million restoration, Scott Tanvir Properties is hosting the Avondon Winter Ball to celebrate his 30$^{th}$ birthday**

- **TittleTattle magazine's Top Toffs of 2017 expected to attend including minor European and Arab royalty, oligarchs, celebutantes, and trustafarians**

*Link:* ***Scott Tanvir ranks #3 on the BritAsian Eligible Men List of 2017***

'Isn't it a bit desperate to travel 6,300 km to blog about a ball and err, meet a blind date?' I asked Ayana, who'd sweetly offered me her family's flat in London to stay in while I was there.

'Hell no!' she retorted. 'The ball will be *super* happening, *yaar*! You know I'd go with you if my cousin's engagement wasn't happening! I'd go based on that invitation alone!' she joked, referring to the beautiful gilt-edged, thick, off-white card that had been couriered over, embossed with the words 'Avondon Park'. A small notecard accompanied the envelope with 'Scott Tanvir Properties' inscribed in silver. Handwritten in blue were the words: *'Can't wait to meet you!—Scott.'*

I wondered how Princey would react if he knew that I was being introduced to Scott. I could just imagine him curling his lip with…disgust? Jealousy? Indifference? Jealousy, I hoped, though I figured I'd never know one way or another.

I headed straight for Ayana's flat in St John's Wood from Heathrow. The key was waiting for me with the doorman. I deposited my luggage in the tiny flat decorated in dove-grey and cream, took a quick shower, and though still exhausted from the flight, left for the salon appointment I'd booked before my departure.

I felt a lot better after a double espresso and a sleek blow dry. My styled hair fell in pretty layers that swished as I walked back to the flat to get ready for the ball.

I shook out a shimmering dress from my suitcase. It had been part of my trousseau. I didn't earn a great deal as a blogger but it came with certain perks, and fashionable attire was one of them. I could borrow from local designers, as long as I could squeeze into their sample sizes — luckily, I was the right height too. Because they knew I was sure to get photographed, I could also order customised styles at a fraction of the prices quoted to the shopping-mad wives of Faisalabadi industrialists.

I finally perfected my smoky eye and paired it with coral lipstick, ending with a dusting of shimmery strobe powder along the bones of my brows, cheeks and collar, and a whiff of Carolina Herrera's stiletto perfume bottle aptly called 'Good Girl' I'd bought at Dubai Duty Free in my jet-lagged stupor. I slipped on the transparent Valentino lucite wedges embedded with crystals that had maxed out my credit card and took a look in the full-length mirror. Not bad, if I may so myself. Loss of appetite following Princey's betrayal meant I no longer had a stomach to suck in at all, and my eyes looked bigger and my cheekbones higher. I felt a nervous shiver at what I was about to do. Best-case scenario – I was going to a ball to meet Prince Charming. But what was the worst-case scenario?

I hadn't had very good experiences with fix-ups so far, usually a complete lack of chemistry. I hadn't had very good experiences with love in general. Before Princey, there were your usual arrogant, swaggering men who thought women were put on this earth to look after them.

The one exception had been an older man from out of town whom I'd met at a glamorous Lahore party. He was suave, well-spoken, and seemed really interested in what I thought about things, all of which was great till I discovered he already had a wife. Turned out he wasn't really interested in what I thought about that.

I had just turned twenty-seven when I met Princey. It was a balmy December evening and I'd been visiting Karachi for the city's snootiest charity fundraiser of the year. The invitation list for the coveted Friends Against Dengue Society was always heavily oversubscribed. The grande dames on the fundraising committee vetted the attendees and only issued invitations if one made the cut—money, breeding, social standing—the usual. That was the whole point of going, really, no riff raff, and friends from all over the world. An unmarried man at such an event came pre-approved.

I had gone with Ayana and we were staying with my college roommate and sister from another mister,

Neha Dukanwalla, who was wearing a slinky black cocktail dress with a cheeky bow on the derriere. I was wearing a colour blocked midi in fuchsia with slim cut-outs on my waistline while Ayana sparkled in a silver Balmain mini worn with a corset belt.

As we drove up to the closely guarded venue that had been revealed just the night before, we were confronted by endless rows of sedans often accompanied by their own protection unit—a pickup truck containing moustached bodyguards holding semiautomatic weapons. It was a private property on French Beach belonging to a textile tycoon; the hosts had outdone themselves with this year's Nikki Beach-inspired theme, organised around a massive sculpted garden and infinity pool overlooking the Arabian Sea. The white marquee billowed and imported white blossoms fluttered in the sea breeze. The DJ spun pulsating tracks on a high platform.

VIP guests who'd forked over the equivalent of thousands of dollars for lounges were placed on a superior level, overlooking the lesser round tables purchased for hundreds of dollars a head. Guests walked in with their BYOB stash and handed it to their allocated waiters. Dukanwalla Cooking Oil was one of the corporate sponsors so we were seated at a fantastic lounge with Neha's parents and their cronies and spent our time discreetly eyeing the plumped and bejewelled glamazons below. Missonis air-kissed Puccis and Cavallis, while Hervé Légers sucked in sagging abdomens. Obscenely large solitaires dazzled on earlobes, throats, fingers, and wrists.

Ayana was the only one under fifty who was thrilled when the hip lounge music turned to disco and she dragged us on to the dance floor. As it got later and later, the music went back to electronic, and the dancers got younger and younger as the night wore on.

It was hard not to notice the attractive man in the lounge next to ours. At 6'3", he was half a head taller than the average Karachi guy; his chiselled face bore Slavic cheekbones. When he started speaking to me, I almost looked around to check he wasn't addressing someone else. But speak he did, was he… flirting? It seemed he was.

My friends poked me and whispered his name. He was quite literally a nawab sahib with princely blood coursing through his veins. His khandaan had moved to Karachi at Partition, and then on to Dubai fifteen years ago. *Architectural Digest* had covered their flashy Emirati villa replete with designer décor and fleet of Skittles-hued sports cars. Princey was educated at Sandhurst which had given him an attractive physique for life, followed by Cambridge. He was given a seat on the board of directors at the family firm, and had dated an assortment of unsuitable models. His mother, who dressed in head-to-toe Chanel, had been a Czech stewardess on British Airways when she had served Princey's father champagne in First Class, and subsequently, went from Stefania to Syma.

I'd smiled that night and flirted along, my nerves allayed by the fact that someone like that couldn't possibly be seriously interested in me. Well, you all know how that went.

As the Uber approached Avondon Park, I gasped. I was expecting a pretty, rustic pile, but this was truly wedding-cake glorious, with a Palladian façade made with Bath stone surrounded by lush manicured foliage.

I joined the queue of guests – in outfits ranging from the merely formal to the bizarre – on a red carpet leading up to the steps. The flash photography was relatively unobtrusive. I hoped this was a good omen – Scott would be dashing, sophisticated, urbane, and gentlemanly, and I would no longer be jinxed in love.

The hall screamed Georgian glamour with its Rococo splendour and art works. I walked along a long gallery and gazed at paintings and sculptures, pausing before displays of exquisite snuffboxes, Dresden china and gleaming silver, before accepting a flute of champagne from a liveried footman. Reluctantly, I tore myself away from the gallery and entered the ballroom, with beautifully high ceilings amid a treasure trove of oil paintings, and pillars of gilt and marble. Guests twinkled among lustrous antique chandeliers, floral festoons, and silver candelabras juxtaposed with modern chrome. Throngs of beautifully dressed Tatler-Bystander types in dapper suits and glimmering gowns chattered. There were discernible Russian, Arab, and Indian cliques.

The women were mostly stunning, but the same couldn't be said of a lot of the men accompanying them, jowly things averaging sixty. A handsome man in a navy blue suit caught my eye and smiled at me. I smiled back and then blushed scarlet, making him laugh. I looked the other way, still flustered. I really couldn't be making eyes at strangers, with a set-up with the heir to this magnificent property in the works.

'Before I met you, I said "*Inshallah*". Now that I've seen you, it's "*Mashallah*",' said an unfamiliar, jocular voice.

I raised an eyebrow and turned to see a young desi man dressed as a Victorian-era Raja. My eye immediately alighted on his strings of seed pearls fastened by a large ruby onto a garish silver-wire embroidered *sherwani*. *Oh, please let it be someone who merely resembled Scott, a master of ceremonies, perhaps? Oh, please don't let it…no, no it can't be…*

'Roya? Hi there. I'm Scott. Welcome!'

It was Saqnain. His eyeline was level with my neckline, which is where his eyes were focused.

'Thank you, Scott,' I said, heart sinking.

I offered a hand but Saqnain awkwardly tiptoed up to kiss my check. That's when I noticed a generous bald spot. Well, I guess if Prince William had one…

'You have an exquisite home,' I said, folding my arms across my chest to encourage him to look up at my face. 'I'm so pleased I was able to be here tonight.'

'Not half as pleased as I am!' he replied. 'There'll be a *bhangra* on soon and I really want to dance with someone who can get the moves right instead of acting like they're screwing on a light bulb.'

'A *bhangra?* At your *ball*? At *Avondon Hall*?' I said, hoping the Gainsborough on the nearby wall couldn't hear us.

'Absolutely. DJ Srilata is here, she's brilliant. Let me get you a drink?'

Without waiting for an answer, he beckoned a waitress who offered us a tray of mini test tubes filled with a green liquid that looked like kryptonite.

'Absinthe,' he smirked. 'Bottoms up!'

I sipped at it gingerly but it was vile. Blagh.

'That's not how you down a shot,' he said. 'Let me show you…'

'Err, no thank you,' I said hurriedly. The last thing I wanted was for Sweetie Aunty to reprimand me for getting plastered and humiliating myself and my loved ones aka *zalaalat*. 'I'd love some Perrier.'

Before the waitress could return with one, the thumping music began and next thing I know, he'd pulled me onto the dance floor and started gyrating to a Bollywood mash-up with Taylor Swift. His hands lurked at the small of my waist as I tried to move away, while also desperately scanning the room. You couldn't walk fifty feet in London without running into a familiar Pakistani, but apparently this rule didn't apply in Surrey.

I found myself locking eyes with the man in the navy blue suit again, speaking to an attractive woman in a backless dress, but looking directly at me with a smile in his eyes.

With nowhere to run, I had no choice but to dance with the one person I knew at the entire ball, the reason I was here. Scott danced with wild abandon, all flailing limbs and comically unrestrained facial expressions. 'Ooooh, lalalala, hai hai hai!' he shouted, along with the chorus, throwing in a pelvic thrust for good measure. I swayed, moving as little as possible, longing for this moment to end. He said something but I couldn't hear him over the music. He reached a hand out to pull me closer to him, he said it again, I didn't hear it, but I nodded anyway just so he'd let go of me.

Could a magnificent estate make up for zero chemistry? The hope that it could flickered and died. I needed to get the hell out of here. I was thinking of an escape plan when Scott executed a Michael Jacksonesque spin and elbowed me right in the boobs. I let out a wail and backed away, mouthing 'excuse me.' Once out of his reach, I practically ran off the dance floor and back onto terra firma. Looking around to make sure Scott hadn't followed me into the panelled hall, I took a deep breath. The set-up had been a disaster but I could still take some notes and blog the party. I could make my return to writing, if not dating.

'You and Scott make such a handsome couple!' a deep voice said. I looked up horrified. It was the man in the navy suit. From up close, I could see that he had classic Hollywood matinee idol features, a straight nose, melting hazel eyes, full lips, and a rather attractive cleft in his chin. His lustrous, dark brown hair was flecked with grey and I could just catch a hint of a subtle, spicy cologne. 'Tell me, what most drew you to him, his dance moves or his reserved demeanour?'

He gave me a crooked grin.

I was about to explain till I suddenly felt rage. Rage at having made this journey, rage at Scott being a total moron, rage at this being how I was spending my wedding day, and rage at a complete stranger, albeit a really sexy one, judging me for dancing with his host.

'There's a lot more to Scott than you seem to think,' I said, icily.

I unconsciously looked over to the dance floor—a space had cleared in the centre where Scott appeared to be trying his hand at breakdance. My heart sank further yet.

Navy Suit laughed again. I started to walk away but he came after me. 'Sorry, sorry!' he said, 'I'm sure Scott is actually brilliant. I don't want to talk about him anyway. Where are you visiting from? You're obviously not a Londoner, with your accent.'

'Pakistan,' I said. I waited for the inevitably tedious response – 'Is it dangerous there? Do you know Malala? Do you know my random Pakistani friend from university? Your English is "so good."' But none came.

'Where were you six years ago when I went hiking to K2?' he said. 'My one and only time there.'

I was impressed. Also, the thought of him hiking made me rather shamefully think of what his torso may look like under his impeccably crafted shirt. 'The most adventurous thing I've ever done is to go to a hill station for a yoga retreat. And then rush back after three days without Wi-Fi!' I said.

He reached over and pushed a strand of hair away from my face. It suddenly felt as though the ball was far, far away. He was close enough to kiss.

Suddenly, I heard a screech. I quickly drew back.

I turned around and saw the last two people I'd ever want to encounter in a dark corner: Emané Ahmed and Harry Gulzar.

Emané was a socialite who attended ladies' committee lunches by day and snorted coke by night. She had ash blonde hair extensions with a bulbous trout pout and was wearing a sequinned Moschino Pepto-Bismol pink mini dress with a crotch-skimming slit that revealed an inch of a Spanx corset. She carried a cocktail in one taloned hand and an Alexander McQueen skull clutch in the other.

Harry was an event planner who hosted pop-up shops and retail launches while paying B-grade models to grace them with their presence. Lacklustre red carpet photos were then sent to glossies all over the country and Instagrammed with the hashtag, #SPOTTED. Harry wore a too-tight Gucci suit in dark teal accessorised with a Gucci belt and pointy

Prada shoes. They were both fixtures on the Lahore social scene.

'Who's *this* hottie?' Emané said in a too-loud whisper.

'*Jaani,* share him with me too,' Harry said, as he produced his selfie stick and captured a group shot before I had even spoken a word.

I was mortified. What must Navy Suit think of this tackiness?

Of course, when it rains, it pours, and soon enough, Scott had reappeared at my side, now sweaty from his dance routine. '*Meri jaan*, the DJ is playing "Laila O Laila" and you know what that means!' *It means the time has come for me to set myself on fire*, I thought.

Ignoring my protests, he literally wrenched my arm across the dance floor. He spun me with such ferocity that I only just righted myself without falling over. If ever there was a time to be grateful for Emané being resolutely socially ambitious, it was now. She sidled up to Scott and whispered something in his ear. He looked at her and giggled. She joined the dance, clearly trying to push me back on the dance floor and install herself in front of Scott. Standing with her legs akimbo, she started shimmying in the most fascinatingly vulgar manner. I took the opportunity to slope off the dance floor again. I looked back and this time, Scott seemed occupied. I breathed a sigh of relief and vowed to never complain about Emané again, at least not till I got to Lahore.

I cast about, hoping to find Navy Suit—I didn't even know his name. I wanted to apologise for the ambush by Harry. Actually, I just wanted to see him again, but all I saw were lots of unfamiliar faces. My feet were beginning to hurt; I think I'd pulled something when Scott had spun me around that last time. It was time to call it a day. I pulled out my phone to call an Uber. I'd not had the opportunity to look at it since reaching Avondon and was alarmed to see that I'd missed a dozen calls from Myra. I walked to a quiet balcony and called her back.

'Royyyyyyya!' She screeched. 'Why aren't you checking your messages?'

'What happened?' I asked, panicked, 'is everything OK?'

'Everyone is talking about how you've snagged the biggest catch of the season! Sweetie Aunty is so proud of herself and so proud of *you*. About how you got Saqnain to run after you, even before his visit here to the Sindh Club Ball and all the rounds with hundreds of girls and their mothers throwing themselves at him! Sweetie Aunty said she heard Princey is mad as hell that you got over him so fast and complaining about you at a party in Dubai. And...'

'What are they talking about? How do they know anything? I'm going to have to call you back, Myra...'

I walked down a corridor and began scrolling through my phone's social media newsfeeds.

670 notifications on Facebook alone. And my Instagram followers had swelled to 200,000+. And then I read why.

**The DailyTale**

- **Halal Burgerland heir Scott Tanvir's 30th Birthday Ball is a smashing success with toffs, zillionaires, and society sirens**
- **Lady Avondon dons £20,000 Avondon Tiara for the first time since the Royal Coronation**
- **Beatrice and Eugenie photographed leaving worse for wear**
- **Scott Tanvir spotted canoodling with blogger Roya Khalil, estranged fiancée of 'playboy' Princey**

**18K** shares

(***Scroll down to view photos of the Best and Worst Dressed***)

This was accompanied by someone's blurry iPhone photo. No wonder! I'd been papped by @HarryGulzarTheBestPR.

There I was, held by Scott's tentacles on the dance floor. In the next photo, his hand was on my waist. *The DailyTale* was virtually getting me married off, thanks to Harry's photo leak that he'd hashtagged #ScottTanvir!

Sweetie Aunty was probably distributing wedding sweets by now.

I felt sick. I put my phone on the stone railing of the balcony and leaned against it to take a deep breath.

'So, you and Scott, eh?' said a voice I'd been longing to hear. I turned around and there he was, the Navy Suit, with that same cocksure grin.

'Yes?' I said, in a challenging tone.

'Well, I was wondering about you and me.'

'You and me?' I said, a shiver passing through me. 'I don't even know your name'.

'It's Olivier', he said. Olivier! It had such a nice ring to it. 'And I'm not currently making out with your friend on the dance floor like Scott', he continued.

*Aah, Emané*, I thought. Sweetie Auntie would be horrified but I was delighted.

'So again,' he said, moving closer, 'I wanted to ask you about you and me.'

Before he could get as close as I'd hoped, a stately lady with a shimmering tiara in her flaxen updo approached.

'Olivier!' she said, in a clipped accent.

'You're with her?' I said, somewhat surprised.

'In a manner of speaking—I'm Lady Avondon's bodyguard,' he whispered.

He straightened and turned to the older lady, whom I recognized as *the* Lady Avondon. She been born a Luxembourgian aristocrat and Lord Avondon had been her second husband. After his death, she'd sold his debt-ridden ancestral property to the Tanvirs and was now enjoying a more prosperous existence. She lived in the Dower House adjoining the Park.

I supposed that Lady Avondon probably wanted to scold her employee for mingling with the guests.

'Ma'am, if I may, it's all my fault,' I said quickly, before an introduction could be made. 'Your bodyguard actually came to my rescue.'

'Oh yes? My *bodyguard*, did you say?' she commented drily, a single eyebrow raised several inches above her faded blue eyes. 'Olivier?' She looked pointedly at him.

My phone buzzed and I excused myself to a corner. It was an attachment from Myra. *'Lucky escape'*, she'd written beneath it. It was Hi Society! Pakistan's Instagram account of Princey sandwiched between a Lebanese model duo, determinedly living it up on what would have been our wedding night.

I clicked my phone shut, shuddering to think I had come so close to having babies with this man. For the first time since the debacle of being betrayed, I realised I wasn't feeling at all hurt. Olivier was walking from the balcony back into the party. It was typical of life that the most attractive man at a party full of wealthy and titled people should be the least appropriate, not even an invited guest. *I would go from Princey to Tanvir the Tycoon to someone's household help*, I thought. *I don't care*.

I never wanted to meet another prince again.

Ever.

DJ Srilata was now playing feel-good eighties music and I could hear it echoing in the terrace. As the chilly outdoor air whipped my hair across my face, I tried to steady my breathing and felt a sense of calm I hadn't felt in a long time.

I wouldn't get married. No more pressure. So, *what* if I got too old to have a baby? I could freeze my eggs. Or adopt. I just needed to find a better paying career. Although after tonight, my social media following had gone through the roof, not a bad thing for a blogger…

Seriously though, no more men who seemed right rather than men who felt right. No more *rishtas*. No more eligible morons! No more following the money. I would make my own way in the world. *I could at least try*, I thought. But first, there was one thing I had to do. I ran inside.

'Olivier,' I called, 'Olivier!' I was shouting now, and I didn't care who heard.

'Were you looking for me?' he said, appearing from inside a knot of people.

'Yes', I said, smiling, 'I was.'

He smiled his crooked smile.

**The DailyTale**

- **Best or Worst Dressed? You Decide! Princess Eugenie, Victoria Beckham, Lily James, Bella Hadid…CLICK FOR MORE**
- **Scott Tanvir seen embracing a Kylie Kardashian-lookalike who has poured her curves into a barely-there dress…**

- **Europe's hottest princelings: Publicity-shy Olivier, youngest son of the Grand Duke of Luxembourg... CLICK FOR MORE**
    - ❖ **Olivier is the entrepreneur of ecofriendly high-rises in Scandinavia and is seen here in close conversation with blogger Roya Khalil, formerly photographed with Scott Tanvir...**

# Acknowledgements

This was a labour of love that wouldn't have been possible without so many people's help – thanks to all Austenistanis and everyone at the Jane Austen Society of Pakistan—we did it! Brown girls REPRESENT!

Thank you to my parents, for always saying yes. To Mahlia and Harris, the most loyal sister and kindest brother a girl could ask for.

To Faiza at Bloomsbury for being her brilliant self and for believing in this project when it was just an inkling of an idea. To Jay at Jacaranda, my kindred spirit and the dearest of agents.

To my family – Auntie, Gasha, Saif, Faiz, Dinara, Rayyan, Soniah, Sarah, Fahad, Sobia, Jahanara, Ana, and all my aunts, uncles, cousins around the world and my late beloved Kashmiri Abaji, Punjabi Abaji, Moji, Ami—you are loved! A special mention to Auntie Helen for giving me my first Austen novels on my 12th birthday, which I will always cherish.

To all my sisters – for you are really nothing less – Rishm, Saniyya, Ayesha, Izza, you kept me afloat. Sweetest, kindest Wajiha, Saba, Sabrina, Munizae, Tanya, Mehreen, Mashaal, Fazila, Fatima, Amber,

Shazo, Rina, Faiqa, Sehyr and all my remarkable friends, well-wishers and loving, supportive soul sisters and brothers – you know who you are and I am so very fortunate to have you all in my life.

To all the wonderful print, digital and broadcast media, friends and supporters around the world who have shared our enthusiasm and excitement, the British Council Pakistan, the British High Commission Pakistan, the Jane Austen Society of North America, the Jane Austen Literacy Foundation, the Jane Austen House Museum, All Things Jane Austen, Factory Films, Muse District, The Last Word, all the wonderful lit fests that have invited us to speak, Moni, Caroline, Joan, Rebecca, Amanda, Ashok, Sam, Basia, Rosemary, Maarya, Adriana and so many, many more – thank you!

And, finally, my eternal appreciation to the incomparable Jane Austen, for enriching my life and for continuing to fascinate and inspire imaginations around the world.

# Biographies

### Nida Elley

Nida Elley is a college teacher, writing coach, and freelance writer based in Austin, Texas, and has been published in journals and publications including *Psychology Today*. Nida received her BA degree in Journalism & Mass Media from Rutgers University and an MFA degree in Fiction Writing from Sarah Lawrence College. She currently teaches Rhetoric and Composition at St Edward's University in Texas.

### Saniyya Gauhar

Saniyya Gauhar is a barrister by profession and was Editor of the Pakistan based business magazine, *Blue Chip*, for four years. Saniyya has worked in corporate law and litigation in both London and Pakistan. She is currently a freelance writer and editor based in Islamabad, and has had articles published in magazines and daily newspapers, and has edited and co-authored papers for prestigious international academic journals.

### Mahlia S Lone

Mahlia S Lone started her career as the Assistant Editor of the Op/Ed pages at *The Nation* followed by a stint as the Features Editor of *The Friday Times*. Based in Lahore, she currently freelances as a textile journalist contributing frequently to publications including *Women's Wear Daily* and works as the Editor of *Good Times* magazine.

**Mishayl Naek**

Mishayl Naek is a freelance writer and economist, formerly at the State Bank of Pakistan. Mishayl lives in Karachi, where she runs the Yummy Mummy Network to address childcare issues, activities and resources for metropolitan Pakistani mothers. She has been published in various print and digital publications including *The Express Tribune, Good Food, Grazia Pakistan, Libas International,* and *Women's Own*.

**Sonya Rehman**

Sonya Rehman is a freelance journalist based in Lahore and has been published by *TIME, Rolling Stone (Middle East), the BBC, The Hindu, The Huffington Post, Al Jazeera, The Diplomat Magazine, Forbes, The Friday Times, DAWN* and *The News International*. She was awarded the Fulbright Scholarship to pursue Print Journalism at Columbia University, where she received the Joseph Pulitzer II and Edith Pulitzer Moore Fellowship. Sonya teaches English and Journalism, runs a postcard start-up, *From Lahore With Love* and organizes local TED events.

She has anchored and scripted for television at HUM TV, hosted a radio show for City FM89, and conducted Journalism and Creative Writing workshops.

**Laaleen Sukhera**

Laaleen Sukhera is a communications consultant and media professional based in Lahore. Laaleen has worked in TV production, advertising, and media projects in Pakistan, the UK, and the USA. She appears as a panelist and public speaker at literary events and on television programmes, and is the founder of the Jane Austen Society of Pakistan. Laaleen is currently working on a novel and a screenplay.

**Gayathri Warnasuriya**

Dr Gayathri Warnasuriya is a scientist and programme manager currently based in Amman, working on science and innovation partnerships between the UK and Jordan. She has a PhD in Molecular Biology and Toxicology. Born and brought up in Sri Lanka, she has been a nomad since the age of fifteen and has lived, in chronological order, in Saudi Arabia, the UK, Nigeria, Guyana, Barbados, and Pakistan.